SO-AZS-151

The
Mystery
=at=
Wolf River

**Other Apple Paperbacks
you will enjoy:**

Secret Agents Four
by Donald J. Sobol

The Mystery of the Haunted Trail
by Janet Lorimer

Ghost Cat
by Beverly Butler

The Ghostmobile
by Kathy Kennedy Tapp

A Ghost in the Window
by Betty Ren Wright

The Mystery at Wolf River

Mary Francis Shura

AN
APPLE
PAPERBACK

SCHOLASTIC INC.
New York Toronto London Auckland Sydney

No part of this publication may be reproduced in whole or in part, or stored in a retrieval system, or transmitted in any form or by any means, electronic, mechanical, photocopying, recording, or otherwise, without written permission of the publisher. For information regarding permission, write to Scholastic Inc., 730 Broadway, New York, NY 10003.

ISBN 0-590-44361-5

Copyright © 1989 by Mary Francis Shura. All rights reserved. Published by Scholastic Inc. APPLE PAPERBACKS is a registered trademark of Scholastic Inc.

12 11 10 9 8 7 6 5 4   3 4 5/9

Printed in the U.S.A.   28

First Scholastic printing, May 1989

1. James

The only mystery in the beginning was how I could have been so stupid. If I hadn't broken the rules and taken my little brother James down by Wolf River, that week would have been just one more cold, wet week in March instead of the scariest and most painful few days of my whole life.

You have to understand that James is more than just an ordinary little brother.

Dogs have fleas. Birds have mites. I have James.

Of course I haven't always had him. Since I am going on twelve, I have put up with James for only half of my life. I was already five when he decided to be born halfway through my birthday party. I *should* have guessed right then what a pest he would turn out to be. The neighbor who took over when Mom went off to the hospital cut the cake wrong and was stingy with the scoops of ice cream.

That March Monday I was even more annoyed with James than usual. It had rained steadily for a solid, sloppy week, keeping me from doing my work for Mrs. Mclaughlin. She lives in the second house down the road from us and I'm in charge of her yard when she's off in Florida. Mr. Frimmle, who takes care of the big Roberts' estate, used to clean her yard, too, but they had what she calls a "falling out." I never knew what they fought about, but after that she called him a "dirty old bandit" and told me if I ever saw him put a foot on her land I was to call the police.

I was really glad when she asked me to take over the yard. I love working in her yard almost as much as I love the money she pays me for doing it. She likes to feed wild things, birds, and raccoons, and even squirrels. She doesn't really *like* to feed squirrels but you can't feed other animals without squirrels coming to eat, too.

There's no point in trying to do anything when it's raining, but when the sky was clear Monday, I planned to go over to Mrs. Mclaughlin's right after school and work until supper time.

Instead, I got saddled with James.

Mom is always reminding me that she would be happy to pay me as much for sitting with James as she pays Cindy Nelson. I'm not *that* crazy about money. James doesn't obey me, he has a head as hard as a bowling ball, and he tattles.

I had just settled James in the family room with cocoa, sandwich cookies, and *Mr. Rogers,* when Bugs came over.

Because we're best friends, Bugs just raps on the door and opens it right up. "Kate," he called, his voice sounding excited.

"In here," I told him. "I'm coming."

He was already inside the door. You have to really like Bugs Moran to enjoy looking at him. Mostly he dresses in grubby chinos and a jacket of the same color, both with mud stains. He wears his baseball cap with the bill sticking out in back and his eyes look huge behind his glasses. His eyes are a really spectacular blue, which is a good thing because otherwise he's completely colorless, with hair that mingles straw color with darker strands. When he smiles he has teeth enough for three kids.

I feel guilty about it sometimes but even though Bugs is my best friend, I'm still glad he doesn't go to my school. I don't mind that he looks weird or that he acts as strange as he looks, but I'd just die if I had to watch the kids at school make fun of him.

I'm older than Bugs by three months but he's so serious that you'd think he was all the way grown up. I've never figured out whether he goes to private school because he's so smart or because his parents have only one kid to spend their money on. They let him get away with what my mom and dad would call "murder." He has a pet tarantula named Gladys, an ant farm, a gerbil named Hamlet, an aquarium with hermit crabs, and an immense black cat named Pitch. When he isn't doing some science project for school, he spends most of his time crawling around in the dirt looking for things with more legs than he has.

In fact, that's exactly what he was doing the first time we met. He was squatting in the dirt in Mrs. Mclaughlin's backyard with a magnifying glass. "What are you doing in here?" I asked, more startled than anything else.

"Studying ants," he said, scrambling to his feet and grinning at me.

"This is private property," I told him. Then what he had said really hit me. "Why would you want to do something stupid like that?"

"What's stupid about studying ants? I'm going to be a biologist, maybe an entomologist. There's nothing wrong with starting early."

I must have shown how much I thought of that because he looked at me in a really challenging way. "So what do *you* want to do?"

That's not a question I like to answer. If you are a kid who wants to be laughed at or put down hard, just tell somebody you want to write books. His sarcastic tone almost goaded me into slipping up and telling him. Instead, I hesitated for a minute.

He grinned. "Are you ashamed or something?"

That got me. "No, I'm not ashamed," I said, trying to make my tone haughty. "I'm going to write mysteries."

That time he laughed right out, acting as if any book that wasn't half filled with the Latin names of insects was junk food for the mind. "What a waste! With the same amount of energy, you could do something useful."

"Make some big breakthrough, I guess. Something like finding something new that crawls?" I asked.

"At least breakthroughs in science are intellectual," he said pompously. "They are made when intuition is supported by research."

"Quit talking to me as if you were educational TV," I told him. "Mysteries are solved exactly the same way."

Amazingly, we got to be friends. Although he's never taught me to like bugs and I've never gotten him to read mysteries, we've stayed friends.

Other people take pictures of people. Bugs takes pictures of wildlife. And taking pictures was what was on his mind that day.

From the way he was grinning, showing all ten miles of those teeth, I knew he had something *he* thought would be exciting to do. (We don't always agree on what's exciting, Bugs and I.)

"What's up?" I asked him.

He chuckled. "It's more what's down. The geese are going north. A bunch of them always put down to feed in those cornfields along the river down by Smuggler's Spit." He patted the pocket of his down jacket. "I've got fresh film. Let's go down and get some shots of them."

"With the river almost up to flood stage from the rain?" I squeaked. All my folks had talked about for a week was the rising river and danger of flood.

"Come on," he coaxed. "We can watch where we're going. There'll be plenty of light until the sun goes down. That's about another hour and a half."

"I can't anyway," I told him. "I'm stuck with James again."

I didn't have to explain why. We both knew that Cindy Nelson, who's supposed to come by after school and watch James, was off somewhere competing in a swim meet. The Nelsons believe that working improves a teenager's character. Cindy isn't sold on the idea herself. Bugs and I have privately agreed that Cindy only went out for swim team to have an excuse not to baby-sit James. The fact that she turned out to be good enough to make the team was *my* bad luck.

James had left the TV to follow me. "I like geese," he said from behind me.

Bugs grinned at him. It's apparently easier to like little rat-faced kids if you don't live with them.

"These are Canada geese," Bugs told him.

6

"I like Canada geese," James said.

"Well, you can't go and that's the end of that," I told him. "You can't go, and I can't go either because I'm responsible for you and you don't mind for thunder."

"I do so mind," he said. Then, at my look, he dropped his eyes and scrubbed his sneaker toe on the carpet. "I mind Bugs. He isn't bossy."

"He *does* mind me," Bugs said. "At least he always has."

James knows better than to nag at me. He just stood there, waiting for whatever was going to happen next.

"Most particularly I'm not supposed to take him down along Wolf River," I told Bugs. "Because of the dangerous currents and all."

"The geese are in those cornfields, not on the water," Bugs reminded me. "They'll be waddling around looking for grain to eat."

"See?" James put in hopefully. "That's not the river, Kate, that's the cornfields." What a little parrot that kid is. He was born able to repeat everything he hears and make it sound as if he understood it.

Bugs stuck out his left arm and squinted at the mammoth watch he got for Christmas. "We won't have much time unless we take off right away."

I studied James a minute, trying to figure out how good my chances were of his behaving himself. They're never all that good. Dad thinks it's great that James has a "mind of his own." Personally, I wish the kid would go along with what anybody suggests, the way most of his friends do. Then maybe we could get him a mind of his own when he's about junior-high age and I'm off in college.

"I *really* like Canada Geese," he said wistfully, looking at me.

In this entire world only Mom considers James an appealing child. He is so skinny that his jeans look uninhabited. His hair is pale and his face comes to a point. His eyes are dark and too big for his face. He lost his front teeth falling off a sled the day he was five. Maybe he'll look better when his smile doesn't look like the Black Hole of Calcutta, but I doubt it.

When people *really* want to make me mad, they say James and I look alike. I may be slender and blonde and brown-eyed, but any possible resemblance ends right there. *I* have visible teeth.

Both Bugs and James stood there silent, just looking at me and waiting.

"Okay, okay," I finally grumbled. "But *you* are going to mind, James Graham, or you'll be sorry for the rest of your life."

2. The Upside-down Boat

I have to give it to James. He didn't even complain about my making him put on thermal socks and wear a big knitted scarf.

The day was typical for March in Illinois, ugly and uncomfortable. Patches of dirty, leftover snow still hid most of the grass and the wind rattled through the barren oak trees that lined the fence around the Roberts' estate. I looked up toward the house, craning my neck to see past the evergreens around the porch. "What are you looking for?" Bugs asked.

"Mrs. Roberts's grandson, Andy Wallace, was supposed to get here this week," I told him. "I keep thinking I'll see some sign of him."

Bugs laughed. "You keep *hoping* you'll see some sign of him. I've never seen the people in this neighborhood as happy as they were when the news came out that Mrs. Roberts had left this place to him in her will."

"It was the right thing to do," I reminded him. "It's Andy's home. He grew up here."

"He hasn't been here much since *I've* lived here," Bugs reminded me. "He didn't even make it to his grandmother's funeral."

"He's an art collector. He was in darkest someplace and couldn't get back. You've seen all those vases and statues in that house. He has to find them before he can buy them."

"What if he sells this place to Ponti Builders and goes back off to darkest whatever?"

I looked at him in horror. "Don't even *say* that. This whole ridge would be ruined." Everybody knew that the Ponti Builders had repeatedly tried to buy the big estate for development. Mrs. Roberts wouldn't even talk to them about it while she lived. She never would have even sold off the land that our house and Bugs's stand on except that her dead husband's brother Clovis Roberts waged a huge expensive legal battle to break his brother's will. That man would probably sell off to Ponti, too. The thought of those acres being crowded with little Ponti town houses made me sick.

"Somebody's loading a truck back there," Bugs told me.

I looked. "That's just Frimmle the gardener. He's probably been cleaning out the yard, which is what I should be doing at Mrs. Mclaughlin's right now."

We slipped and slid on the ice all the way down Ridge Road and crossed over into the cornfields. Nobody has ever built on that land because it floods too often, but it's rich and fertile and produces giant corn crops.

Wolf River changes with the seasons just the way the woods along our ridge do. Some winters it freezes so solidly that people cross it on foot or cut holes and sit all day ice-fishing. In the summer it's beautiful, almost dreamy, as it flows along quietly on its way to the Mississippi. It has narrow gravel beaches and a dock we swim from at the city park. People can even rent paddleboats and take their chances out there with the water-skiers. Closer to Northville, where the land is lower, a lot of big houses have been built along its banks by people that Dad says like to bail water out of their basements.

He says that because in the spring Wolf River really gets out of hand. When we get big rains or the snows melt up north, the water flow picks up speed. The beaches disappear and the river rushes and plunges along, sometimes leaping out of its banks and over the levees our town puts up. The water washes things away, too; boats stored on private docks, even charcoal grills left out on decks. These all go tumbling along downstream among the logs and debris the river has carried down from up north.

It's only a few yards from the end of our road

11

to where Smuggler's Spit starts to jut out into the channel of the river. It's a big triangle of land with corn planted on it right down to the water's edge.

We got there right away and left the road to walk through the field. The geese were scrounging in among the snow patches at the base of the dead brown cornstalks. They were huge creatures with brown wings folded over their big, heavy bodies. Their necks and heads were black but the band of white running under their heads and up their cheeks made them look as if they were wearing bandages for toothaches.

I have no idea how many were in the flock but there seemed to be hundreds of them. They apparently hadn't heard us coming because they went on scratching and scraping and honking companionably among themselves. Bugs turned and pressed his finger to his lips to warn James and me to be quiet.

I wanted to laugh. The geese were making more noise than we'd ever be able to — unless we shouted. I squatted beside Bugs as he started taking pictures. I love to watch him work with his camera. He gets himself into the most ridiculous positions, leaning and crunching down, and frowning fiercely. All the while, he bites on his lip nervously as if somebody's life or death depended on that particular shot.

I didn't notice when James left us. One minute he was squatting beside me staring at the geese and the next minute I heard him calling me.

"Sissy!" he shouted, his voice strange and panicky. "C'mere quick!"

That did it.

The geese, all of them, honked alarm and took off in a wild clattering of heavy wings. The air blasted downward, almost blowing me backward on my heels. They circled in panic above us, wheeling and honking. I covered my ears against the hollow wooden clatter of their wings and scrambled to my feet, blazing with fury at James.

"All right for you, James Graham!" I called. Not only had he ruined Bugs's picture-taking, but my name is Kate, and he knows it.

I looked around the cornfield for his orange watch cap, feeling a moment of panic. I've jumped on him so many times for calling me "Sissy" that he only uses that baby-talk name in a real crisis.

"James," I called again. "Where are you? What's wrong?"

His voice came from far away, clotted with tears. "By the water. Hurry!"

Bugs had stowed his camera gear in a few swift movements and was crashing through the cornfields after me. Even though lots of the stalks had been bent or knocked down by the snows, they still concealed the riverbank from our view.

"Keep calling, James!" Bugs shouted at him. "We can't see you."

"It's going to be too late," James wailed.

Bugs and I broke out of the corn rows about twenty feet upstream of James, just where the spit of land curves out into the channel of the river. James was running along the frozen riverbank following an overturned boat. He was waggling a cornstalk at it. The current was carrying the boat too swiftly for James to reach it with his stick, if it would have done any good.

"Jeepers!" Bugs whispered, passing me like a shot. He reached James, shoved him back into the cornfield and said, "Stay here," before taking off after the boat himself.

Only then did I see why James sounded so desperate. An animal of some kind, big and black and slimy, with only its nose out of the water, was paddling desperately in the wake of the boat. I caught up with James and turned him around so his head was against me and he couldn't see that poor, struggling dog fighting for his life. "Bugs will get him," I told James. "Quit bawling. Bugs will get him."

But Bugs wasn't getting him.

It went through my mind that the dog had to be crazy not to leave the boat and swim to shore. Then I saw a bright streak of color surface by the dog's head and disappear again. It was a leash!

The animal was *tied* to that boat. If he didn't drown, he would be battered something awful by the big logs and debris swirling around him. I couldn't stand the thought. I really couldn't stand it.

3. Smuggler's Spit

I shoved James down between the frozen cornstalks and growled right in his face. "You
move from this spot and I'll eat you."

His eyes had white all around them as I took
off, running after Bugs.

I'm no powerhouse but I can run fast, and I
have strong arms from tennis. I've tried fishing
things out of that river before and I knew we
needed some kind of a hook. Before I even
reached the river edge I saw a sturdy forked
branch coming toward me downstream. It looked
big and heavy enough to be of some use.

Bracing myself as well as I could with nothing
firm to hang onto, I grabbed for the floating tree
limb. And missed. The second time I caught it,
but barely. With the force of the water carrying
the limb along I felt as if I had taken on Wolf
River in a tug-of-war. I could just see myself
being tumbled over and over in that icy stream.

I was just about to give up when I managed to get a firm grip on the limb.

I ran backward from the bank, dragging that big clumsy branch after me. I fell once but managed to get back on my feet without breaking anything. I ran out on the spit after Bugs, dragging the forked branch after me.

"Good girl," he yelled, glancing back at me. "Hurry up, the boat's coming in."

Sure enough, the current was nudging the craft nearer to the north bank of the spit. The trick would be to catch it before the current snatched it back into the main channel.

I shoved the big wooden limb at Bugs. "The leash," I yelled to him. "Snag his leash."

Bugs stared at me stupidly for a moment, then grabbed the limb and stuck it out over the water. Somebody should have had a camera on us. We were both running, with Bugs lunging toward the boat with the stick every few yards. He was smart enough not to drop the limb into the stream too soon. He ran too good a chance of being dragged in after it or losing our only possible tool.

The rowboat jerked and spun in the water, swinging the tied animal our way. Bugs dropped the limb between the dog and the boat and snagged the leash on the first try. I wanted to whoop with victory but it would have been too soon. When the limb caught on the leash it almost jerked Bugs toward the water. I grabbed him around the waist and held on like bloody murder.

Bugs grabbed the loop of leash snagged on the limb and tried to pull the animal to shore. He got as close as the dog's head when the boat was caught by the current again.

"Hang on," Bugs screamed. The dog yelped in pain as Bugs jerked the collar over the animal's ears. Bugs grabbed for the animal but the dog yelped again and disappeared under the surface of the water. As he did, the boat was caught by the current and went spinning around the end of the spit and on downstream.

As I gasped, that black nose broke the boiling surface of the water again and the animal paddled desperately toward us. The stream kept tugging him toward the end of the spit and the main current. Finally he made it. Less than two feet from the end of the spit he clawed himself up on the bank and collapsed there, panting desperately. Bugs and I glanced at each other before running over to him.

By the time we reached him, he was reviving. He looked up at us with wide-set, dark brown eyes. His tail dragged back and forth a little as if he would have wagged it if he'd had the energy. He was coal-black except for a white blaze between his eyes, and he was immense. I guess I had thought he was a Labrador until he got out on the bank, but he had a dense, longer coat than a Lab has, and his fur had a little curl in it.

Then he struggled to his feet and shook himself, sending what seemed like buckets of water flying in all directions.

I squawked and backed off but Bugs went right up to him. "Here, fellow," Bugs said, offering his hand for the dog to smell. When the animal didn't bare his fangs, Bugs patted him and murmured something comforting I didn't catch.

"He's huge," I whispered to Bugs.

He nodded. "He's a Newfoundland. He probably weighs as much as both of us together."

"But he's all right?" I asked.

"Now can I move?" James wailed from back in the cornfield where I had shoved him down.

"We're coming," I called to him, staying beside Bugs who was coaxing the dog to follow. When we reached James, the animal was shivering wildly, and the water dripped from his sturdy, straight legs into pools around his feet.

Then Bugs patted the dog's head. The animal whined and turned his head away. "He has a big lump there on the right side of his forehead," Bugs said. "We're lucky we got him out before he was hurt any worse."

"Look at him shake," James wailed. "He's freezing."

"That's just to warm him up." Bugs droned on

to James with one of his little science lectures. He finished with, "Newfies can take a lot of cold water, but he must have been in there quite a while."

"The man got away," James said.

"What man?" Bugs asked.

"The man who had the dog in the boat," James said, putting one arm across the dog's shoulders. "He's mine, isn't he? When you save a dog, you get to keep him."

I stared at him. "*You* saved him?"

"Well, sort of," he said, looking at Bugs for support.

Bugs is as accustomed as I am to the funny way little kids think. "Well, he wouldn't have been saved if you hadn't seen him," Bugs conceded.

As Bugs spoke, the air turned suddenly colder. It does that when the sun falls behind Roberts' Ridge. The sun sinking behind the ridge meant it was almost time for Mom and Dad's train to get in.

"Home," I said sternly to James.

The dog padded, dripping, along beside us. We were all wet and cold. It's always a lot farther going up than it is going down. I looked down at the dog. "Now what do we do?" I asked Bugs.

"Try to find his owner," Bugs said.

"Do we really have to?" James asked. "I want a dog. I *need* a dog. I could just keep him."

I've listened to James beg and whine and plead

all my life. Since I can only be so wet and cold and still put up with that kid, I set off climbing the hill faster. James would listen to Bugs better than he would me anyway. Right away I was far enough ahead that all I could hear was the faint rhythm of their voices. I didn't care what they were talking about. I was too worried about what my folks would do when they found out I had taken James down to that river.

The street lamps were on, and light shone from windows all along the street. At least I had beaten Mom and Dad home. Our house was as dark as the Roberts' house, which had been empty since Mrs. Roberts died. The safety timer Mrs. Mclaughlin sets when she leaves for Florida made her house look lived in, too. But there was still the problem of that massive beast standing there, looking at James almost eye to eye.

"James," Bugs said thoughtfully. "How about I take the dog home with me tonight?"

"But he's my dog," James wailed. "I've always wanted a dog just like this one." He hooked his arm around the dog's huge furry neck as he spoke. The animal thumped him cordially with his tail.

"The only way he can be your dog is if we can't find his owner," Bugs told him. "But we've got a fenced yard at my house, and my folks won't care."

"My folks won't care," James began, and then

looked at me. "Probably they won't care," he added in a squeezed, discouraged tone.

"Then it's settled," Bugs said, squatting by the dog. "Tell him good night, James."

James clung to the dog's neck, fighting tears, and mumbled, "Good night." He flew inside to keep us from seeing that he was crying.

"What are the chances of your folks letting him keep the dog?" Bugs asked. "That is, if we can't find the owner."

"About one in ten million," I told him. "That might fall to one in ten thousand if he weren't the size of a horse."

"What's with your folks and animals, anyway?" Bugs asked.

"Mom is into Clean with a capital C," I told him.

He chuckled. "And she takes humans over other animals? I guess she doesn't travel on Chicago's el train."

I watched Bugs start off toward his house at the end of the street with the big animal padding along beside him. While I was still watching, Bugs turned and said something to the dog. The animal looked up at him and responded with a graceful wave of his tail.

I felt a slice of something like guilt. James loves animals as much as Bugs does. I had blamed our not having pets on Mom but that was only half of the truth. When James had begged for a dog on our last birthday Dad said we could get one if I would be responsible for taking care of it.

"I'm not the one who wants a dog," I told him.

"Then I guess we have to wait for some growing up to happen," Dad had said, turning away without looking at me again.

4. The Broken Levee

I turned on the lights and started my homework. I couldn't think of any other way to make points against the ones I was going to lose when James told Mom and Dad about going down to Wolf River. As it turned out, the traffic crossing the Wolf River bridge was really slow that night. Mom and Dad were so late getting home that I had finished my homework and had the table set before they finally got in.

Mom looked really tired. She came in without smiling. Her mind seemed a long way away as she hung up her coat and pulled on her apron. Then she went straight to the refrigerator and took out a package of shrimp. I silently groaned. Because they both work, my folks run what they call an "equal opportunity" household. They split all the jobs. They divide cooking chores the way they do everything else. That gives James and me an equal chance of having slaw every other night. When Mom does the main dish, Dad makes salad. Since he can only make cole slaw, we are really cabbaged out!

Dad put his arm around Mom and snitched a piece of carrot from the paper towel where it was drying. She slapped his hand and he went back to scraping carrots for the food processor.

"You're awfully quiet tonight, Kate," Dad said to me.

"And cooperative, too," Mom added, looking at me in a funny, solemn way. "Did you see that table already set?" she asked my father.

What could I say? Understanding your parents is a lot more important than even fractions. You can get tutoring in fractions but no one can ever explain parents to you. I don't know whether Mom is moodier than Dad or whether I can just read her better. I knew she was distracted and whatever she was thinking about bothered her. She was not in the best mood to hear that I had taken chances with her little darling James. Even though my stomach was empty, I still felt a hard knot in it.

Before I could say anything, James came thumping down the stairs dragging that hideous green stuffed frog that he's hauled around ever since he was a baby. He was wearing his sleepers, his duck-bill bedroom slippers, and a grubby wool bathrobe I'd forgotten he had.

"Look at *you!*" Dad said. "You can't be ready for bed already!"

Mrs. Scheller

"I was just cold," James said, sliding up onto one of the breakfast stools. He set the frog on the counter and rested his chin on it.

I could feel it coming. He was going to tell them about Wolf River.

Instead, James looked at me, licked his lips, and said, "I was even shivering today."

"We all do that sometimes," Dad said absently.

"Do you know why animals shiver, Dad?" James asked.

Dad grinned at him, apparently thinking this was a riddle. "No, James," he said dutifully. "Why do animals shiver?"

"It's a form of exercise," James recited. "By flexing their muscles, they raise their body temperature."

Mom and Dad both turned and stared at him. "Where in the world did you learn that?" Mom asked. For once she appeared simply amazed instead of openly delighted with her child's brilliance.

"From Bugs," he said, rolling his dark eyes toward me.

I don't know what came over me. Something about James's look filled me with despair.

He was toying with me.

He *knew* I shouldn't have taken him down there by Wolf River. He *knew* he could get me in trouble whenever it suited him to tell Mom and Dad about it. The thought of going through my entire life waiting for him to drop this one on me was too much. I caught a quick breath and glared at him.

"Bugs and I pulled a dog out of Wolf River today," I said, louder than I meant to. "He was tied to a boat and would have drowned if we hadn't saved him. He shook like a leaf when he got out on the bank."

The jerky grinding of the food processor stopped abruptly. Mom lifted the strainer of shrimp from the oil and set it on a platter. The kitchen was absolutely quiet except for the sizzle and pop of the boiling oil. They both turned to stare at me.

"You *what?*" Dad said.

"I heard her," Mom said quietly. She wiped her hands on her apron and walked over to me. Somehow she seemed taller than usual standing there looking down at me. "You children went down by Wolf River without any grown-ups along? Where on Wolf River?"

"Not far," I said, beginning to feel cold inside. I didn't want to mention exactly where because the swirling currents around the spit are supposed to be the most dangerous on the river.

"Smuggler's Spit?" she asked, her voice beginning to waver.

I nodded. Then, in the hope of changing the

way this was going, I added, "Bugs said the dog was a Newfoundland."

Dad stood looking at me with a strange expression I couldn't name.

Mom turned away. She lifted James down from the stool and patted his behind. "You go watch TV a little while," she told him.

"But I'm starving," James protested. Mom pulled a handful of cookies out of the jar and thrust them into his hand. "Eat these. Dinner won't be long."

I stared at her as James thumped his frog behind him off into the family room. This was a first. Never before in my life had I ever seen Mom give either one of us a sweet before dinner.

Then I was there alone with the two of them. "How many times have we told you not to go down by that river, or to take James there, without an adult along?" Mom asked.

"A lot," I admitted, not able to meet her eyes.

It would have been easier if she had yelled at me. Instead her voice got very low and tight and painful-sounding. "I think I would feel better about this if you could give me some reason why you went."

It whizzed through my head that I could say that Bugs Moran had talked me into it. That wouldn't have been true and it wouldn't have been fair. I had argued against it a little at first but in the end, I went along of my own accord.

"I didn't have any reason," I told her.

Then she lost control of her voice, "Where is your head, Kate? What were you thinking of? You know the river is rising. That's all you've heard since last week. The river is rising. The levees!" She had begun to cry without apparently noticing it. But the tears coursed down her face, making little pale tracks through her makeup. Her whole body was trembling, and her hands were whitened fists when Dad came over and put both arms around her.

"Go upstairs a while, sweet," he whispered to her. "I'll talk to Kate." She stood stiff in his arms a moment before melting and letting him lead her to the door.

My arms were so tight against my body that the bones in my chest hurt. It really hurt to have him standing so close to me without even reaching out a hand.

"Whatever you do, Kate Graham," he said slowly. "Don't ever forget the pain you just saw in your mother's face."

"She'll never forgive me," I whispered.

"She'll forgive you but she won't ever be able to forget it," he said. "You see, Kate, your mom was already upset from hearing the news on the way home. The levee broke in Northville this afternoon, sending that river coursing right through town. It happened almost without warning. Both people and cars got swept away. They are still trying to figure out if everyone is accounted for."

I stared at him, trying to imagine the river roaring through that little town I knew so well. I *knew* people there. Some of the kids in my class lived in Northville: Cassie Thomas and Ben Fremont, for instance.

Dad was looking at me but he didn't seem to be seeing me. "There's a report, so far unconfirmed, that Andrew Wallace was a casualty. He was last seen in the parking lot of the inn about the time the levee broke."

"Casualty?" I whispered, not really believing what he was saying. "Our Andy Wallace? Mrs. Roberts's grandson?"

He nodded. "He had apparently just arrived at the Olde Gray Inn. There was naturally a lot of confusion when the levee gave way. After that low area there by the river was evacuated, they couldn't find him."

"But a casualty?" I asked.

He shook his head. "They were searching the river when we finally got across the bridge."

I buried my face in my hands, trying to hold back my tears. No wonder Mom had been so furious with me. Maybe James could have been swept away by the river, too. Mom was never

ever going to trust me again. Dad pulled me against him and patted my back the awkward way he does.

I shivered against him, thinking of those big logs rolling end over end as they swung around the curve of Smuggler's Spit.

5. Foul Play

Dad put on one of Mom's aprons and finished the shrimp. I made the rice and cooked frozen peas by the directions, but I couldn't think about anything but Andy Wallace.

In the olden days this whole ridge belonged to the Roberts family, as well as most of the land on our side of Wolf River clear to Northville. They built that big fancy house and the stables and carriage house out back. When Mr. Roberts died and his brother Clovis tried to take away Mrs. Roberts's money, she sold off enough land to build the other five houses on the ridge. Even though she was the richest person around anywhere, she was really nice. She was a warm, round kind of woman with a lot of white hair that she grabbed back into a scarf when she went outside. She liked kids and used to have Easter egg hunts and serve ice cream and cake afterward. I can't say I really knew Andy Wallace because he was at least twice my age, maybe more, and always went away to a special school. But he always made his home with his grandmother, Mrs. Roberts, right there on the ridge by us. By the time James was born, Andy went off to college and then to Europe to learn more about the rare kind of art that he collected. I only saw him from a distance. He always looked very tall and thin and drove a red convertible, when all the other cars on the hill were dark colors and sensible.

"Doesn't he have any parents?" Bugs asked the first time he saw Andy home visiting his grandmother.

I shrugged. "All I know is what I've overheard," I told him. "His mother was really sick before he was born, and died when he was just a baby."

"What about his father?" Bugs asked.

"I guess I never heard anything about him," I admitted.

When I asked Mom about Andy Wallace's father, she looked over at Dad for help. I knew right then that I was going to get only half a story. It isn't that Dad is into confusing me but when something is hard to explain, Mom always gets Dad to do it.

He sighed and looked thoughtful for a minute. "His father went into the service and died in Vietnam. Andy was already living here with his grandmother when he died."

"It's funny his father didn't want him," I said,

really shocked that a father would go off to war instead of taking care of his son.

"Andy never was a really healthy child," Mom put in. "His grandmother had better resources."

When I looked puzzled, Dad laughed. "By that your mother means that Mrs. Roberts is filthy rich. Sometimes it takes a lot of money to raise a child with health problems."

That conversation had taken place two years before, when Bugs first came to the ridge. Until the night the levee broke I hadn't thought about how sad Andy's homecoming would be. The thought of being made an orphan two whole times made me shiver.

By the time Dad and I together got dinner on the table, Mom had come back downstairs. She didn't look at me or say anything to me, which made me feel cold again and shut out. We were still eating when the policeman came to the door. I heard him tell Dad that the Morans had called to report the dog that we had pulled from the river.

"I thought I'd check for details," he told Dad. "We're following every lead we can get on the flood loss this afternoon."

"No word of Andy Wallace yet?" Dad asked.

The policeman shook his head. Then he fished a notepad out of his pocket. "We're trying to get in touch with all the people who left messages for him at the Inn."

"Surely there's no suspicion of foul play," Dad said, clearly astonished.

The policeman frowned. "We're just following leads. Maybe you know these names." He looked up at Dad. "Jason Hardaway?"

Dad nodded. "You should locate Jay easily enough. His law offices are right in Northville. He was Mrs. Roberts's attorney."

"Gunther Frimmle?" the officer asked.

Dad smiled. "I'd never heard his first name before. He's always just been called Frimmle. He's a gardener who's worked for Mrs. Roberts ever since we moved here. I have no idea where he lives. He always just comes and goes in his truck."

The officer flipped through the pad and put it away. "Then the builder, Ponti." Dad nodded but didn't say anything.

James and I had both followed Dad out into the hall. I should be embarrassed to admit that I stared at the policeman as rudely as James did, but I was really interested, and anyway I had a genuine reason. If I intended to grow up and write mystery stories, I would have to describe policemen for my readers. I see crossing guards all the time but I usually only see policemen from a distance, when they pass along the street in their cruisers. Like Bugs holding his magnifying glass down for ants, I was studying this specimen.

This man was younger than a crossing guard but older than most of the policemen on TV shows. He was tall enough to make Dad look short. His hair was curly gray and untidy from the cap he pulled off when Mom opened the door for him. He looked very solid, as if he had been stuffed into his uniform jacket after it was buttoned up. The smell of leather came into the hall with him, probably from his boots and holster. He had a nice smile with wrinkles on both sides of his mouth, but his eyes didn't look very happy. He introduced himself as Captain Logan.

Dad told James and me to go back to the table and finish eating. I was still nervous enough about disobeying rules to be obedient. James went with me all right, but he didn't intend to miss anything. He sat down and made an absolute hog of himself. He scooped big gobs of food off his plate into his mouth. He didn't even chew. He just swallowed, choked, and crammed his mouth full again. A girl could get sick just watching him eat. In no time at all his plate was empty. He slid off his stool and shot off into the living room after Mom and Dad.

It must have been all right because after just a few minutes Dad came to the door and asked me to come in there, too.

Captain Logan looked at me very strangely. "We've been talking to your brother," he said.

"I'd like to hear your version of what happened this afternoon."

I looked down at the floor because I didn't want to meet either Mom's or Dad's eyes. I told him about going to the cornfield for Bugs to take pictures of the geese.

The officer nodded and made a note on his pad and looked up. "This is Bugs Moran?"

I nodded. "His real name is Victor Moran."

"They named him Victor before they knew he was going to be a runt," James put in. I winced. Bugs says that about himself but I wasn't sure he would be thrilled to have James announce it to the world.

Dad put his hand on James's knee. "Don't speak up again unless Captain Logan asks you to," he told him.

I went on and Captain Logan didn't interrupt me again until I told him about making James stay back in the cornfield.

"And you threatened to eat him?" he asked. I looked at him, startled. Then I saw the wrinkles around his mouth twitching and smiled back.

"James is really hard to threaten," I explained. Mom's sigh was faint, but I heard it.

Until Captain Logan started asking me about the boat, I didn't realize how little I had noticed. I thought it was gray, a regular metal-gray rowboat like a lot of the ones along the river. I didn't see oars. I didn't see any letters printed on the boat, which would have been upside down anyway.

"And the dog was fastened to the boat?"

I nodded. "It was dragging him along by a regular leash."

"What do you mean by regular?"

"A leather leash fastened to a collar," I explained. "Bugs almost tore the dog's ears off taking off the collar so the dog could get free. The current was awful," I added. "The dog already had been hit bad on the head. We didn't have time for anything."

Captain Logan made another note. Then he closed the notebook and stood up. "If you think of anything more, just call, will you?"

I nodded. James was bouncing straight up and down on the footstool, about to explode. Captain Logan looked at him and grinned. "The same goes for you, young man."

"The dog belongs to somebody who can't hear," James said, with a guilty glance at Dad. "He's a Hearing Ear dog."

Captain Logan stared at him, then frowned. "Why do you say that?"

"His collar and leash were orange," James said, with a sidelong glance at Dad.

All of us were staring at the kid but only Dad spoke up. "What makes you think that's what an orange leash means?" he asked.

"Bugs told me."

Captain Logan shook his head. "Clearly I need to talk to this Victor 'Bugs' Moran."

I think I just sat there with my mouth open. The leash *had* been orange but that hadn't meant anything special to me. Hearing Ear dogs were just the kind of thing that Bugs always managed to know about. That must have been what he and James were talking about while I shivered up the hill ahead of them.

After the policeman left, Dad insisted on taking my turn at the dishes. I told him I didn't mind because I'd finished my homework. Mom answered before he got a chance. "In that case, young lady," she said, still not looking at me, "you get your clothes off and get into bed. This has *not* been one of your better days."

The minute I settled down in bed I started crying without really knowing why. Was I crying because I was sorry I'd been so irresponsible? Or because my parents (and James) deserved a better person than I was?

I was almost asleep when I heard the soft thudding sound. It took me a minute to realize it came from lumps of snow being thrown against my bedroom window. I went to look out. Of course it was Bugs. He made elaborate gestures as if he were a professional mime. I opened my window and leaned out.

Bugs is wonderful! As usual, he had figured

everything out in advance. He poked his fishing rod up to my window with a note hooked to the end. When I caught the note safely, he waved cheerily and trudged off.

From his handwriting you'd think Bugs hadn't made it through the second grade, but the message was clear enough. Three things. I was to tell James that the dog had eaten a good dinner and was fine. I was to meet Bugs halfway between our houses at seven-thirty the next morning. The third was strange, all in capital letters. *SOMEBODY SAW A MAN IN THE BOAT WITH THAT DOG. NOW YOU'VE GOT YOUR FIRST MYSTERY!*

6. The Search

Naturally it started to storm during the night. Along with cold we get spring storms, black clouds, thunder and lightning, and torrents of rain.

Roberts' Ridge isn't the best place in the world to be during a storm. It's a craggy and wooded cliff that runs into the forest preserve in back. The wind howls in from the southwest, rattles our shutters, and bends our trees. Really *bad* storms, the ones with gale winds, pick up debris and branches and trash from the forest preserve and dump them in our backyards. Mom and Dad bought our place for the great river view without thinking about storms or how hard it would be to get home in the winter when that winding road was covered with snow or ice.

By seven the next morning, the wind had died down. It had been replaced by a fog that looked like a sea of milk. I groped my way through it to the halfway point, which is between Mrs.

Mclaughlin's house and the old Roberts mansion. When Bugs didn't get there right away, I began to feel cross. Fog is spooky because you can't see even the normal things. Even ordinary sounds become muffled and ominous. Anyway, what could possibly be important enough to bring me out into the cold this early?

I danced up and down, humming out loud to myself to keep warm while I waited for Bugs. The van sneaked up on me. Since the driver didn't have his lights on, the purr of the van's motor was right behind me before I knew it was coming. I dived into the ditch in front of Mrs. Mclaughlin's house, barely making it out of the road in time.

I hate being scared. I hate having my breath come in short gasps and feeling as if my joints are melted. I scrambled back onto my feet but was still brushing snow off my jeans when Bugs appeared out of the mist.

"Take a spill?" he asked, looking at my clothes.

"Spill!" I repeated. "No way. That stupid van almost ran me off the road."

"Van?" he asked, his expression really blank.

"Don't give me that," I told him. "It had to pass you on the road."

"Nothing passed me," he said. "Not so much as a low-flying crow." Then he nodded, looking wise. "It must have turned into the Roberts' drive."

"Why would it do that?" I asked. "Vans don't go to houses where nobody lives."

He frowned and stared at me. "Maybe that gardener who takes care of the place got himself a van."

"Mr. Frimmle?" I asked. "No chance. That van looked practically new. Mr. Frimmle is a famous tightwad. He's the Ebenezer Scrooge of gardeners. He wires the broken handles of his shovels together and tapes up holes in plastic bags so he can use them over and over."

Bugs had screwed his face up in thought. "I know the van you mean. It's painted blue and has those dark, clouded windows."

"Sure, Bugs," I said. "You just described it, but you didn't see it."

"Not this morning, but I've seen it here before. There's a little printed sign in the front window that reads 'Elite Cleaning Service.' "

"Why would a cleaning service come to an empty house?" I asked.

"Are you kidding? Kate, that house is full of artwork and expensive furnishings. That sort of stuff has to be taken care of."

Sometimes Bugs is too logical to be likable. "I'm freezing," I told him. "Why did you drag me out and almost get me run over?"

"Did you watch the late news?"

I gave him a look. He knows my parents better than that.

"Okay, okay," he said, nodding. "They're launching a search for Andy Wallace in the river,

43

because somebody called the police and claimed he saw a man in a boat with a dog."

"We didn't see any man."

"I know," he nodded. "But this caller told the police he did."

I shivered. "Do they think it was Andy Wallace?"

"Nobody knows for sure. But since Andy Wallace arrived at the inn and then disappeared, they naturally wonder if it was him. Anyway, they're going to search the river. That policeman was hoping there would be some identification on the dog. Of course there isn't, not with his collar gone. The reporters kept referring to Andy Wallace as 'the heir to the Roberts' millions' as if that had something to do with his disappearance."

"That makes me cold all over," I told him.

"Yeah, I know." Bugs's voice was quiet with hurt. Then he looked up at me, his bright blue eyes luminous behind his glasses. "Do you remember what James said about the man getting away?"

I shook my head. "He didn't mean anything by that."

"I didn't think he did either, back then," Bugs said thoughtfully. "But after hearing the news, I've wondered if he really saw a man."

"Surely he would have said something more if there was a drowned man out there bobbing along," I protested.

"All James cared about right then was saving the dog," he said. "That's why I asked you to meet me. We really need to find out exactly what James saw."

"James is not famous for being cooperative with me."

"You can try, anyway. I won't have a chance with him until after school. Anyway, why shouldn't he tell you?"

"If you remember, he was down there running along the bank where he wasn't supposed to go. He's not about to talk to me about that. Think about it, Bugs. There's no way James could have seen the river from where he was supposed to stay. He's not tall enough to see over those cornstalks. Remember how much trouble we had finding him when he was yelling?"

Bugs sighed. "Maybe you're right. Anyway, see what you can do. I'll talk to him tonight."

James always sits behind me on the bus. I made him get back there the first day he started school because I was so cross at him. Other first-graders *know* they're still little squirts. They show the older kids some respect (and sometimes terror) and they don't put on airs. James had to start off the first day of school as if he were as old as I am. He had to have a jacket in the school colors. Mom even bought him a little backpack, even though he didn't have anything to carry in it.

I almost asked him to come up and sit with me that morning. Then I decided I didn't want to talk to him on the bus. I would wait until we got to school where we wouldn't be overheard.

By then it was too late. As the bus let us out on the school grounds, the first of the helicopters swung in low from the southeast, heading straight for Wolf River. The second one came right after it. The cold, foggy air throbbed from the steady drumming pulse of their rotors.

Our principal, Mrs. Thompson, finally herded the kids inside. She managed to get her students all crowded into the hall, but she couldn't quiet them down.

"Ladies and gentlemen," she called in a modified shout. When that didn't work, she clanged the cowbell she keeps for crises.

Grabbing that moment of silence, she explained that the search for the missing man would probably go on all day. "Nobody in this school gets to go home until his or her work is done," she added, glaring around with her most ferocious expression. "If you still want to be here tomorrow if the helicopters come again, just keep up this chattering."

All the kids fell silent except James, who had been shoved back against the office door. "The man got away," he piped up.

Mrs. Thompson frowned and peered over at him. "Why do you say that, James?"

With every single kid in school staring at him, James was overwhelmed. Instead of answering, he turned around, so that his face was against the door, and mumbled something.

The kids who were closest to him started giggling. Finally one of them spoke up. "James says the man got away because only the dog was left in the boat."

Mrs. Thompson, who can be a pretty nice person, smiled in that disbelieving way. "I see. Thank you, James."

I groaned inwardly. Once James turns his back on a question, you aren't going to be able to pull an answer out of him with pliers. If James knew anything more about the man in the boat, only Bugs would be able to get it out of him.

All day long everyone at school wanted to talk about our rescuing the dog. Every single teacher leaped at the chance to lecture us on how dangerous Wolf River was, and how we should all stay as far away from it as possible.

By the time the dismissal bell rang, the helicopters had swayed on downstream so far that they looked like shadowy dragonflies on the horizon. But as the bus crossed the bridge going toward the ridge, wide flat boats with divers were still working the stream. I shivered at the thought of some dead human being nudging the bottom of the half-frozen river.

When I glanced back at James, I realized he

hadn't even noticed the divers. He was sitting with his head back against the seat, smiling to himself. When he saw me looking at him, he leaned forward so close that I could smell the peanut butter from his lunch. "I get to see my dog when I get home," he whispered. His face glowed so happily that, even without front teeth, he was almost attractive.

7. The Ridge

The minute the bus stopped in front of our house, James was off and running south down Ridge Road. "Come back!" I yelled. "Where are you going?"

"To see my dog," James said without even looking back.

"You can't do that," I called. "Bugs isn't even home from school yet."

James paused and stood staring at me a minute.

"Come change your clothes, and get something to eat," I said, trying to coax him. "By the time you finish that, Bugs will be there."

He hadn't moved. "Bugs has a cat," he told me.

"What does that have to do with anything?" I asked, genuinely confused.

"Bugs wouldn't leave my dog inside the house with his cat," James explained. "He'll be out in the backyard." With that he was off again, running along the frozen road with that empty book bag slapping against his thin little back.

I didn't even bother to check the garage for the key. I knew Cindy Nelson was already in the house from the dull thump of the stereo going full blast. All the time Cindy is supposed to be watching James, she either listens to music or talks on the phone with one of her friends. Usually she doesn't even look up when I come in, or put down the phone if she's gossiping. That day she must have been listening for me because she came to the kitchen door.

"Isn't he with you?" she asked, her tone hopeful. Cindy would never admit it but I know she feels the same way about James that I do. Maybe she dislikes him even worse because she never says his name. I may scream it but at least I can force the word "James" out of my mouth.

Cindy must be fifteen because she's a sophomore in high school this year. She's probably pretty to people who didn't see her before she began to mess up her looks. She used to have a nice quick smile and wore her dark hair loose and shiny down her back. Now her hair is all short spikes in front and long and tangled looking in back. She makes up her face to look like a rock star, and she pouts instead of smiling.

"James went down to Moran's," I said, getting out milk and then putting it back. I felt bleak and cold inside from hearing the helicopters all day and seeing the men diving for somebody who had drowned. I put some water in the teakettle and turned it on to make instant cocoa.

"If I'm not needed here today, I have lots of homework," Cindy said, looking hopeful again.

"He'll be back," I told her. "I'm not going to stay with him. I have to start cleaning up Mrs. Mclaughlin's yard."

"That's an even worse job than taking care of *him*," she said, and went back into the family room.

I had finished my cocoa, changed into my grungies, and was almost to Mrs. Mclaughlin's house when Bugs's school bus groaned up the hill. His hand was a pale waggling shadow waving at me through the dirty window of the bus. Then he jumped off and caught up with me.

"Any news?" he asked without even saying hello.

I shook my head. "They were still searching the river when my bus crossed the bridge. James went down to your house to see his dog."

Bugs frowned. "I better hurry then. There's no way he can get inside the fence without a key. I'll be back right away."

I took my time getting the tools out. I had just finished putting a fresh bag in the trash container when Bugs came banging in through the gate. "Is James here?" he asked. He was panting as if he'd run all the way down Ridge Road.

I shook my head. "Wasn't he at your place?"

"He and the dog are both gone," he said.

I dropped the rake. "But I thought you said he couldn't get in there without a key."

"He couldn't," Bugs gasped. "Nobody could. But there's a fresh hole under the fence in back, where the dog must have clawed his way out, and no sign of either of them."

I felt that sudden heavy feeling that comes when I'm really tired or discouraged. "Somehow or another, this is going to end up being my fault," I said. "What am I going to do? I don't know where to start looking."

"James can't have been gone more than half an hour," Bugs reminded me.

"How long did it take him to get into trouble yesterday in the cornfield?" I asked. My tone sounded acid, even to me.

Bugs's expression changed. He tightened his lips together as if to hold his own words back and looked at me squarely through those big glasses. Then he spoke very carefully as if he were reciting something he had memorized. "Put that stuff away while I let the police know the dog is gone. I told them I'd be responsible for him. Then we'll just look for him until we find him. This ridge isn't all that big."

"The little monster," I muttered.

Bugs acted as if he didn't even hear me. He

turned and started off toward home at a jogging run. I shoved the stuff back in Mrs. Mclaughlin's garage and ran home.

It was just as I feared. The stereo was still booming and Cindy hadn't seen a sign of James. "You could come out and help us look for him," I told her.

"How would I know where to look?" she asked. "Don't forget, I haven't even seen him today. Anyway, somebody needs to be here in case he comes home."

"His *name* is James," I told her angrily.

She stared at me with her eyes wide, and coiled some of that twisty mess of hair around her finger. "I know," she said as if daring me to say anything more.

I slammed out of the house and down the walk. I wanted to stay mad at Cindy so the scared place in my stomach would go away.

All your life your parents tell you what's dangerous.

Stay out of the road! (I thought of the blue van and how close it had come to hitting me.)

Stay away from the river! (I saw those big logs tumbling over and over in the current.)

Don't ever go into the forest preserve alone! (I thought of a verse about kids lost in a wood and covered with strawberry leaves, and wanted to cry.)

In fact the only way I could keep from crying was to take a few steps and then call, "James!" as loud as I could.

When you're listening for someone to answer, you notice all sorts of sounds. Squirrels rattled in the branches of the trees along the road, and some bird kept repeating the same notes over and over. I even heard traffic noises that sounded distant and somehow mournful rising from the Northville bridge across Wolf River.

The window curtain twitched as I passed the Lathrop house next door to us. The Lathrops are both really old. They're so old that they even knew Mr. Roberts, who died before I was born. I had almost passed the house, still yelling for James, when the significance of that moving curtain registered on me. Mrs. Lathrop is the nosiest person on the whole ridge. She wouldn't miss very much of what passed on the road. She might even have seen James. I shot up to the front door and rang the bell.

I could tell Mrs. Lathrop had seen me coming from how quickly she opened the door. I didn't waste any time on pleasantries but just asked right out if they had seen James.

Mr. Lathrop appeared behind his wife in the door, grumbling. "It would be a wonder if we hadn't. There's been nothing but traffic on this street lately. You'd think we lived on Main Street downtown. Take today! That Ponti fellow was up here in that big black car of his, and didn't you say you thought the silver car belonged to Maggie Roberts's lawyer, Jason Hardaway?" he asked, turning to his wife.

I groaned. "But did you see James?" I asked, trying to interrupt.

It didn't work. "That was Hardaway, all right," Mrs. Lathrop nodded. "What a nice man he is for a lawyer. He was such a comfort to Maggie Roberts during her last days."

"And that no-good Frimmle went rattling by about noon," Mr. Lathrop went on.

"But no little boy in an orange cap?" I asked.

"Not since he went running by here from the school bus," Mrs. Lathrop said, finally getting the idea. "My gracious! I hope you find him."

By the time I had thanked my way out of their house, Bugs was waiting in the street. "I've been all around our place and the Nelsons'," he said. "There's only the Roberts' estate left."

"And the forest preserve out back and the cornfields and river down below," I added bitterly.

He looked at me again in that strange way.

"Why don't you just go on home, Kate?" he asked quietly. "I'd rather look for James all day and all night by myself than put up with your nasty temper for ten more minutes."

I stared at him, feeling my face begin to swell the way it does when I'm going to bawl. "He's my brother," I wailed.

"I know that. I should probably send him a sympathy card," Bugs said, turning to start toward the gate of the Roberts' estate.

I ran after him. "I'm sorry, Bugs," I said when I caught up. "I'm just scared."

He ignored my apology. "You start calling, your voice carries better than mine."

It's about a half a block all uphill between the Roberts' iron gates and the front of the big house. The drive is a circle with another drive going out toward the back, where the carriage house and stables are. A lot of the trees are some kind of evergreen whose branches grow so close to the ground that they rest on the tops of the snow drifts. Squirrels chattered at us, and a rabbit leaped from a mass of shrubs to hopscotch off around the house.

Mrs. Roberts liked kids. I've played on that porch lots of times while she and Mom visited. For a long time she had a cross old Shetland pony that used to belong to Andy. Her house man, whose name was Mr. Toby, used to put me on the pony and walk him around the grounds when I was really little. All those years I've loved this place and suddenly it was scary. The trees and the looming house muffled my voice, making it sound strange. I went up on the porch and looked into one of the side windows. It took me a minute to realize what was different. Then I yelled for Bugs to come. My cry startled some pigeons from under the eaves. They flew out making so much noise that my heart battered the way their wings did.

Bugs came running up the steps. "Look in there," I said. "Look what's happened."

He whistled softly. "The covers are gone."

None of us are really supposed to mess around up at the Roberts' estate but one time right after Mrs. Roberts died, Bugs and I cut through the place on our way to the forest preserve. I don't know why we went up and looked in the windows, but we did. I've never seen anything so spooky-looking in my life. The place looked haunted. All the furniture was draped with white. In the parlor those pale mounds looked like a congregation of ghosts waiting in the half darkness for life to come back to those rooms. But now the covers were gone. The tables shone with polish and the rich blues and the reds of the upholstery were beautiful even in that dim light.

"And the other stuff," I said. "Where are the vases and the statues?"

"They could have been put away for safety," Bugs said, still staring inside. "Look. The camels are still there. Maybe they were too heavy to move."

He was right. The ancient statues of camels, one standing and one kneeling on its knees, still filled the alcove beyond the fireplace.

"Who do you suppose has been in there?" I asked.

"You said Andy Wallace was expected," he reminded me. "Maybe the cleaning people were told to get the place ready."

I shivered. "It's spooky. It looks as if somebody is living here."

"Well, it's not James," he said. "Let's try out in back."

When Bugs and I reached the fence that separates the Roberts' land from the forest preserve, I looked back at the house. A thin wavering of smoke rose from one of the big stone chimneys. I grabbed Bugs's arm. "There *is* somebody in there," I whispered. "The heat is on."

He scoffed at me. "Of course the heat is on. Do you think they want the pipes to freeze? Doesn't Mrs. Mclaughlin leave her furnace on when she goes off to Florida?"

He was right, of course. Then Bugs started shouting James's name to give my voice a rest.

Even though it was almost pitch-black up there behind the stables, light still glinted on the face of the river, which I glimpsed through the trees.

"You know we have to give up soon," Bugs told me. "If he's not back home by now, we have to get help."

I didn't argue but started back down the hill with him. By that time I was afraid of so many things that I didn't know what scared me the most. I was afraid of where we were, to start with. The Roberts' house, even the outbuildings, seemed to be listening to us whisper and move past them. I was afraid that we weren't going to find James until he hurt himself some way or got lost for good. I was afraid of my mother's face when she heard that James was missing.

The street lights came on as we reached the front gate of the Roberts' estate. "I'll walk you home," Bugs said.

"I'll be okay," I told him.

"I want to know about my friend James," he said, making me feel about two inches high. Suddenly I was afraid of a third thing.

If Bugs decided he didn't want me for a friend, I would simply curl up and die!

Our porch light was on. Cindy popped out of the door before we even started up the front walk. "He's here," she called, waving both her hands. "He's here okay."

I felt a sudden surge of anger. All that fear, all that yelling, and he'd been okay all the time. "He went straight to his room," she added as we got to the door.

"When did he come in?" Bugs asked her.

She shrugged. "Just a few minutes ago."

Bugs whistled softly. "That was close. Did he say where he'd gone?"

Cindy had her books and cassettes gathered up,

ready to go home. She gave Bugs that wide-eyed look she always gives me. "I didn't ask him," she said and let herself out the front door.

Bugs stood at the bottom of the stairs and called up to James. When no answer came, Bugs asked. "Can I come up and talk to you?"

"No," James shouted. "Not now, not ever. I hate you."

Bugs looked at me, his face all wrinkled up. "What's that about?" he asked in a whisper.

I shrugged, and made a try. "James, get down here this minute and apologize to Bugs."

The door slammed so hard that I could feel it through my feet. Bugs's face reddened. He turned to me and whispered fiercely, "You stay out of this, hear me?"

He took the stairs two at a time, and I followed him. He stood outside James's closed door. It was very quiet — too quiet — the kind of spooky quiet I had felt up at the Roberts' place.

"I'm sorry your dog got away," Bugs said to the closed door. "I never thought about his digging his way out under that fence."

When no answer came, Bugs sighed and tried again, "The police know he is missing. They're looking for him right now."

I heard the little groaning sound our garage door makes when it opens and knew that Mom and Dad were home. James must have heard it, too, because he opened the door. He had on that same awful getup he had worn the night before. He squeezed past us to get into the hall, being very careful not to look at or touch either Bugs or me. His face was all red and something like dry sticks of grass were caught in his hair.

"Hey, James," Bugs said gently. "This isn't like you."

James turned on the top step and looked back at us. "I'm different," he said. "*Now* I'm different."

He can't really pronounce that word. He says it as if there weren't any "e" in the middle. It really got me for him to have such a grown-up, cold look on his face and still be talking baby talk.

8. The New James

The minute Mom and Dad got into the house, Dad went straight into the family room and turned on the TV. "Excuse us, kids," he said. "Your mom and I need to catch the news."

Mostly I watched Mom. I hadn't had a chance to tell her how sorry I was about taking James down to the river. The longer I went without telling her, the harder it was going to be. At least she was speaking to me. She glanced at the table I was setting and nodded. "Thank you, Kate," she said without much expression at all. She pulled her apron out of the drawer and went to the door of the family room. She stood there silently watching and listening while I finished setting the table.

Listening was enough to give me cold chills.

They hadn't found any bodies in the river, but they had pulled up a rental car near the end of the flooded parking lot of the Olde Gray Inn. The records showed it had been leased by an Andrew

Wallace of Northville, Illinois. The address he had given was the Roberts' house on our road.

I went to stand by Mom. "Is there anything else I can do?" I asked.

She stared at me vaguely, then nodded. "Put on the big pot of water for pasta. You know which one." She didn't even say thanks but turned to watch the announcer, who was holding a microphone for the manager of the Olde Gray Inn.

"Mr. Wallace had a guaranteed reservation for Sunday night. He received several calls before he finally arrived sometime Monday afternoon. He didn't check in, but apparently set his bag inside the lobby door and went back out to his car. That was just before the levee broke and the river came boiling into town. Everything was terribly confused from then on, but one of the staff members thought they saw him working with his car in the flooded parking lot while the water was still rising. A lot of guests raced out to move their cars to higher ground. None of the staff have seen him since."

Mom and Dad listened while the reporter continued to talk. He pointed out that they might never have found the car if they hadn't searched the river for the missing man.

The spaghetti water was boiling when Mom came back into the kitchen. I had set the pasta out and was grating the Parmesan cheese. This time she did say she was sorry for not helping.

"I'm the one who should apologize," Dad said, "It's my night to make dinner. Want me to do salad?"

"No, no," I protested. "Let Mom do it."

He grinned and took the cheese grater from me. "At least I can finish this. Thanks for the help. Run along and play or something. We'll call you."

I didn't want to "play or something." I wanted to know more about Andy Wallace disappearing. All this time I had thought I really liked mysteries. Suddenly I realized that I only liked mysteries in books. This was a *real* mystery, and I sure didn't like it.

"I refuse to believe that anything has happened to Andy," Mom said, almost angrily. "I won't believe it, as a matter of fact. When I think of what a nice kid he always was, and how hard Maggie Roberts worked at giving that child a decent life, I could just cry!"

Mom turned and saw me listening in the hall. "I thought I heard your father excuse you, Kate," she said without smiling.

I didn't even want to leave my room to go downstairs when they called me for dinner. Everyone was quiet, making conversation in little spurts when the silence got too heavy. I realized at once that James hadn't been kidding Bugs. James was changed that very night. He was so quiet while we were eating that Dad tried to draw him out.

"How was school?" he asked.

"All day there were helicopters," James told him.

"How's the dog getting along down at the Morans?"

I held my breath. James didn't even look up, he just slid his spoon across his plate to pick up more of the spaghetti that Mom had chopped up really fine for him. "He dug out from under the fence and ran away," James said without any expression in his voice at all.

Dad gave me a startled look. "Bugs reported it to Captain Logan," I told him. I could tell Dad was surprised that James wasn't more upset about the dog being gone. I was surprised, too, but I was suspicious along with it. I had a funny little niggling feeling that James was up to something I hadn't figured out yet.

Dad looked at James for a long, quiet moment but apparently couldn't think of anything else to say.

The next day was Wednesday. Half of the week was gone, and I still hadn't cleaned even one of the beds in Mrs. Mclaughlin's backyard. All it would take was one really warm day and the daffodils and crocuses would be pushing those dead leaves up, and the flowers would be ruined from not getting a chance to grow right. Fortunately Cindy was already there to stay with James when we got home on the bus. I didn't waste any time but changed out of my good clothes and went straight down to Mrs. Mclaughlin's.

Bugs came just as I unlocked her door to get out the garden tools. He had his camera swinging around his neck.

"Geese again?" I asked.

He shook his head. "I thought I might take some pictures here and finish off this roll."

"It's too early for ants," I told him, and he grinned. I always tease him about never taking pictures of anything with only two legs.

I stepped inside the garage just as I always do. This time, instead of just grabbing the stuff and going on out, I stopped dead still. A really funny feeling hit me. I didn't smell anything or hear anything. It was just that the place felt strange, as if it were trying to tell me something. I looked around warily.

"What's the matter, Kate?" Bugs asked from behind me.

"I don't know," I told him. "It feels funny in here."

"Is anything missing or changed?" he asked.

I looked very carefully. "That bag of kibble for the raccoons could be in a different place," I said, not sure of it myself.

"Maybe you threw something against it when

we tore out of here in such a hurry last night," he suggested.

When I shook my head, he stood very still, frowning behind those owlish glasses of his. "Can't you give me any better clues?" he asked.

I shook my head. "It's just not right somehow."

"We could call 911," he suggested.

"And tell them what?" I asked, trying to pretend I thought all this was funny. "That I'm spooked just because we found a half-drowned dog, and a man I know has disappeared, and the tool room doesn't feel right?"

He laughed.

"Come on," I sighed. "It's probably just something in my head."

Bugs hung his camera on a nail just inside the door and stood staring at me a minute as if I were invisible. When I waved my hands in front of his face, he looked startled.

"I was just thinking," he said.

"Obviously," I replied. "But about what?"

"I wish I had read some mysteries when you told me to," he said. "Then maybe I could do a better job of figuring this out."

I waited, knowing how Bugs tells you things carefully, instead of just spilling them out and changing them later the way most kids do.

"The mystery began with the flood in town," he went on. "That boat was just like the ones always tied up there along the docks near the

Olde Gray Inn. That was the last place anyone saw Andy Wallace. Somebody tied that dog to the boat and was seen going downriver with him. Was the man in the boat Andy Wallace, or was he someone else?"

"Who else would he be?" I asked. "It's Andy who's missing."

He nodded. "But Andy is coming into a lot of money. Maybe somebody did something awful to him to get his money and tried to escape by boat, then got drowned himself. I think what we need is suspects."

"Andy had appointments," I remembered out loud. "At least three people knew he was going to be there at the Inn."

When he just waited, I reeled them off. "Mrs. Roberts's lawyer, Jason Hardaway, was one. Frimmle and the Ponti Builders also left messages for him."

"Jeepers," Bugs said. "That's more suspects than we need. Every one of them could have a motive."

"For a kid who doesn't read mysteries, you sure have the words down pat," I told him. "What motives?"

He shrugged. "Maybe the lawyer has embezzled money from the estate. Everyone on this hill has some bad name for Frimmle. They call him a pirate and a bandit and words like that."

"That's just because he trades his old tools for their new ones," I told him.

"Maybe he traded something worthless for something really valuable and was afraid Andy Wallace would discover it. We *know* how much the Ponti Builders want to get hold of that property."

"Getting rid of Andy wouldn't mean they could get it."

"Who else would care enough about it to protect it?" he asked.

Since I couldn't answer that, I started taking down the yard tools. "What about the spooky feeling in here?" I asked.

"If we understood that, we'd be halfway home," he said.

"Well, I'm *never* going to get through to go home unless I get started," I told him. Bugs helped me haul everything out into the yard. I started raking under the crab apple tree while he pulled the dead leaves off the bulb beds.

The crab apple tree is the only one in the yard, and it is right spang in the middle. It not only dominates the yard, its shadow keeps any real grass from growing underneath it. It's the untidiest tree you can imagine. Things hang from it everywhere: little tubular bird feeders, wooden shelves like tree houses for elves, and tiny birdhouses with openings too small to get your finger in. Altogether, there are seventeen bird feeders. I ought to know. I've filled them often enough. Wrinkled little knobs like shrivelled apples were always thick on the uneven, moist earth under the tree in the spring, and the air smelled of mold.

After we filled all the bird and animal feeders, I started watering the faint nudging of grass coming up by the fence. Bugs got up and tiptoed to the garage for his camera.

I knew right off what he was after. Filling the bird feeders rings a silent dinner bell somewhere back in the forest preserve. Birds appear from nowhere to flutter and squawk around the newly filled feeders. Two cardinals came, a bright one and a dusty-looking female. Some tiny little birds I didn't recognize just settled in to eat, but the black-capped chickadee only took one seed at a time. He didn't come back for more until he had finished eating that.

I was glad to see Bugs stand up and wind his film. I was tired and dirty and already thinking about hot cocoa at home.

"Want to come over for cocoa?" I asked Bugs.

"Just for a little while," he said. "I'm not going to be comfortable until I make peace with James."

I made the mistake of giving him a look.

"The kid didn't ask to be born," he said, starting off down the road without me.

9. Going It Alone

I caught up with Bugs, and we walked silently down Ridge Road to my house. Cindy's music was thumping away when we let ourselves in. While I started the water for cocoa and looked for cookies, Bugs went off to find James. I couldn't find any cookies anywhere, not in the jar, not on the pantry shelf, not even in the freezer, where Mom never thinks I'll look. I gave up and wrote "cookies" on the memo pad by the phone.

Just as I set out the graham crackers that Mom uses to make piecrust, Bugs appeared in the kitchen door.

"James isn't here," he said quietly. "Cindy said he went down to keep you company at Mclaughlin's."

I stared at him, stunned, while the teakettle whistle rose to a scream in the background.

"You know he wasn't there," I said. "Why would he tell her a thing like that? What's going on with that kid?"

Just then Cindy wandered in with her coat over her arm. "Since you're home, I think I'll take off."

"You might as well," I began, all ready to tell her off for not watching James. Then Bugs shook his head at me and I shut up.

Cindy went on out, but before I could say anything, I heard her voice again just outside the door. "Oh, *there* you are. If you hurry, you could get cocoa."

Bugs went to the door and held it open. James didn't even look at us but walked straight through the kitchen and started upstairs.

I set our cocoa cups on the bar. "Forget him," I told Bugs. "He'll be okay."

Bugs, still by the door, turned and looked at me. His eyes blazed with anger. "What makes you think so? Would you be okay if you lived with a sister who treated you like dirt and a baby-sitter who wouldn't even say your name? What if you only had one friend in the whole wide world and that friend lost a dog you thought you might be able to keep?" His voice ended up high and squeaky and not sounding like Bugs at all.

I guess I had never seen Bugs that upset, and I just stared at him. He grabbed awkwardly at his jacket front, buttoning it up. Then he was trying to get out of the door but couldn't get a grip on the knob with his mittens.

"Listen, Bugs," I began.

"You listen yourself, Kate Graham." His voice

almost sounded as if he might cry. It went up and down and he caught his breath a lot. "I don't know how I ever got to be friends with you anyway. You're mean, that's what you are. Mean and selfish. You don't care about anything but your own skin. James is just a little kid. He could be going to some really dangerous place for all you know. All you care about is that he gets back so you don't get into trouble."

"Bugs," I broke in, wanting to explain.

"Shut up," he said. "Just shut up and don't talk to me. I'm going home where I have *real* friends, Hamlet and Pitch and Gladys."

I just stood and stared after him. I didn't even follow him to the door. That's the first time I ever remember needing to laugh and cry at the same time.

The crying was the biggest because Bugs was right. Nobody ever was very nice to James except Mom, and she's at work most of the time. And I *hadn't* really cared where James was as long as he got home before the folks did. The laughing part, which caught in my throat and hurt, was who Bugs thought his real friends were, as I said.

Hamlet, who is a gerbil.

Pitch, who is a big tomcat.

Gladys, who is a tarantula.

The laughter didn't last very long. When it went away I felt all emptied out and dismal. I slumped on the stool and drank both cups of co-

73

coa, first mine, then his. A girl who has been rejected in favor of a big black spider whose feet feel like eyelashes, is very cold inside.

I pretended to do my math but my head wasn't in it. I kept remembering how cold and quiet and polite Mom had been to me since I took James down to the river. I kept hearing Bugs's voice calling me "mean."

I wasn't mean, I was just sick of James, too sick of him to care where he was going. Bugs was just plain, old-fashioned crazy. What kind of dangerous place could James be disappearing to? He had come back, hadn't he? He had come back safely two whole times.

None of my math answers checked but I put away my math book anyway. I needed to apologize to Bugs if he'd let me. I stared at the phone a long time before picking it up to dial Bugs's number. Instead of a dial tone, I heard a man's voice. I was so startled that I didn't even catch what he said. There was nobody at home except James and me. James *never* called anyone on the phone. Before I recovered, the phone was put down with a little click.

I flew upstairs. James was coming out of Mom's bedroom, where the phone is. When he wouldn't look at me, I grabbed his arm. "Were you using that phone?"

He shook off my hand and kept walking. "This is my house, too," he said.

"But who did you call?" I asked.

Instead of answering me, he slammed his door shut, and I heard the lock click. I stared at the door a minute, then went downstairs and dialed the Moran number. Bugs's mother answered on the fourth ring, sounding a little breathless. "Oh, hi, Kate," she said. "Forgive my panting. I just walked in the door. Bugs's dad took him down to pick up a roll of film or something. Shall I ask him to call you?"

I told her not to bother and set the phone carefully back into the cradle. By the time Bugs got back I would have lost my nerve. I didn't have to apologize anyway. I could *show* him I cared about James. I'd also show Bugs Moran that James wasn't in any danger, but was just running off like that to scare people. All I had to do was find out where he was going.

The way Bugs had kept repeating "mean" stung in my mind. Not only would I find out but I'd do it without the help of a weird, funny-looking kid who played with spiders.

I finished all the graham crackers. The crunching must have cleared my head because the answer just came to me.

James was spending his time with that dog.

I didn't have to solve any mystery. I didn't have to worry about where Andy Wallace was and why his rented car was in the bottom of Wolf River. All I had to do was find that big black dog and I would know where James was hiding out. And the only way to find the dog was to watch James and let him lead me to it.

The second idea didn't come to me as easily as the first one had. In fact, I didn't figure out how to follow James without his seeing me until during math class that next afternoon. From the minute I thought of it I couldn't wait for school to be over so I could go home.

Mrs. Mclaughlin kept her second-best bird-watching binoculars hanging inside her pantry door. I'd pretend to go down there to work, get the binoculars, and keep watch on James from a distance.

Naturally Cindy was late, and I had to stay until she came. Since the snow was all gone off the roads, James got his bike out and rode up and down the street. I watched him a few minutes and went inside to wait for Cindy.

"It's about time you got here," I told Cindy when she came in.

"Big deal," she said.

"James is out on his bike," I told her.

"I saw him," she said, dropping her stuff on the counter. Then she stood with her hand on the kitchen phone, just waiting for me to leave so she could call somebody up.

James was pedaling in front of the Lathrop

house when I passed and waved at him. I told myself that he didn't wave back for fear he would fall off but I knew that wasn't the reason.

As I went up Mrs. Mclaughlin's drive, I saw a glint of blue through the trees at the Roberts' place. It registered that the cleaning people had come again and Andy still hadn't been found. I went on around in back where we hide Mrs. Mclaughlin's key. It was under a different rock from where I usually put it but I didn't think much about it. I had been so tired and cold when Bugs and I left the day before that I was lucky I got the key put away at all.

It felt funny to be going into the house to borrow something. Even though Mrs. Mclaughlin always tells me to make myself at home, I never really do. I only go in to use the bathroom, get a drink of water, or take a snack break from the boxed cookies she leaves in the fridge for Bugs and me.

The funny, spooky feeling I had the day before was back, stronger than ever. I stood in the door of the kitchen a long time before I got up my nerve to go in.

Standing there I noticed things I hadn't seen before. Everything was dusty, but that was normal since Mrs. Mclaughlin had been gone for almost three months. There was a mud streak on the floor by the fridge that I didn't remember, but then I hadn't looked that carefully before. I could have even put it there myself. I tightened my shoulders and went to the pantry.

The binoculars were hanging where I remembered, just inside the door on the right. The pantry looked really neat with almost everything cleaned off the bottom shelves. The only things left were things like oatmeal in a box and dried noodles.

I thought about grabbing a handful of cookies out of the fridge to eat on the way, but decided to get out of that place as fast as I could.

I stood hidden just inside Mrs. Mclaughlin's garage door and peered up the street to locate James. I spotted him wheeling past the front of the Lathrop house again. He was all hunched over on his bike with that silly backpack sticking up like the hump on a buffalo. He got as far as the Roberts' gate and turned to wheel back. Maybe he wasn't even going anywhere. Maybe I was going to stand there all afternoon watching him wheel back and forth.

If I was going to do that, I wasn't going to do it hungry. I let myself back into Mrs. Mclaughlin's house, grabbed a waxed paper package of Fig Newtons from the fridge and went back outside.

James was gone.

10. The Phone Call

With the cookies crammed in one pocket and the binoculars in another, I shot off down the street. I figured I'd check our house for the bike first. James is not a child of iron. He had already been riding out there a half hour at least. He could have gotten cold or tired or thirsty.

I never made it home. I saw the bike rammed in under the shrubbery at the front of the Lathrop yard. I made the mistake of glancing at the house. Mrs. Lathrop waved at me from the front window and instantly opened the door.

"Kate! Ho, Kate!" she called cheerily. "Come up and sit a spell."

"I can't," I called to her. "I'm looking for James."

"He was here a minute ago," she said. "He must be around." She had pulled a fringed shawl around her shoulders and was coming down the walk. "I really want to ask you what you think."

I knew what I thought.

If I didn't escape from her in about two seconds flat, I didn't have a chance of finding out where James had gotten to.

Then she was right there, so close that I could smell the faint carnation scent of her perfume. She was whispering as if we were surrounded by enemy ears. "Surely you've heard your parents talking about this Andy Wallace business, dear," she said. "What do they think happened? Mr. Lathrop thinks that somebody has done Andy Wallace in for his money. He just can't decide which of them it is."

I just stared at her. "Which of whom?" I asked, realizing at once it was a pretty silly sentence. I wouldn't have asked at all if I had guessed she was going to say almost the same exact thing that Bugs had.

"Well," she looked off into a tree where a cedar waxwing was chipping away. "We've all heard about those lawyers who mishandle people's money. Who knows that Jason Hardaway didn't submit to temptation? Maggie was old and trustful. And that light-fingered Frimmle. He once took a brand-new trowel from my toolshed and left an old bent, rusty one in its place. I can tell you that was the last time he tended *my* garden. Who knows what he's found to steal up at the big house? It's probably not in his best interest to have Andy come home and take stock of things."

I stared at her. Why hadn't I thought of that before? I didn't care about any old garden trowel, but what about the artwork that had disappeared from that house? What if it hadn't just been put into storage but had been stolen? She broke into my thoughts, gripping the front of my shirt, and whispering fiercely right into my face. Her breath did not smell like carnations.

"And don't forget that rogue Clovis Roberts. That man moved heaven and earth to try to break his brother's will. He would have left Maggie and the boy without a penny if he had had his way. Chances are, if anything has happened to Andy, Clovis will inherit all this property in a court of law."

She caught her breath as if to gain strength for another whole series of accusations. All this time I was completely losing track of James.

"My brother," I said, raising my voice in protest, but she cut me off.

"Where *does* he get all that energy?"

I heard the squeak of James's wheels before her words were out. I turned to see James wheeling down the road as if he were being chased. He didn't even glance our way, but shot on up our drive, threw his bike into a snowbank, and banged into the house.

As I stared after him, Mr. Lanthrop appeared at the door, fussing at his wife to come inside the house or get a coat on. I made my excuses and ran down the street after James. I had never seen that little kid look so terrified in my whole life.

By the time I got to the kitchen door, James and Cindy were already at it. I guess I just stared for a minute. James doesn't mind me, but he has never been known to stand up to a grown-up in hand-to-hand combat.

The two of them were struggling over the kitchen phone.

"Please give me the phone," James begged, hammering on her with one fist and tugging on the cord with the other. "I got to make a call. I got to."

Cindy tried to jerk the cord away from him. "Shut up and go away," she yelled at him. "Can't you see I'm using the phone? Stop it, this instant."

"Please, please," James begged, straining for the phone she was holding too high for him to reach. "It's important. I have to have it."

Cindy turned her back all the way on him, "Pay no attention to the little monster," she yelled into the phone to her friend.

"Hang up," James shouted. "Oh, please, please hang up."

He was crying. Tears poured from his eyes and his voice was thick with sobs.

I've never had the world's best temper, but I

couldn't remember being that mad. Who did she think she was, anyway, treating the kid like that?

I reached for the phone but she was too quick for me. "Give James the phone," I told her. "Hang up and give James that phone."

She started to laugh for the benefit of her friend on the line. "Hear that? Now *both* of them are pestering me. Didn't I tell you how perfectly awful — "

James stood, tears just pouring out of his eyes and his arms pressed tight against his sides, staring at both of us.

"You need the phone, James?" I asked him.

He nodded, splashing tears onto the collar of his polo shirt.

"You want the phone, you got it!" I said.

The big red pot that Mom cooks spaghetti in was upside down on the drain board because it doesn't fit in the dishwasher. I grabbed it along with a big metal spoon out of the pitcher by the stove. I stayed just out of Cindy's reach and began to bang on that pot as fast and loud as I could.

She screamed and tried to cover one ear with her free hand. "Stop that!" she yelled. "You little monster!" She grabbed for me and got her hand in the way. I didn't care how hard I hit it. I was aiming for the pot, not her hand. This time the scream was for real. She said something tearful into the phone and hung it up to turn on me.

I held the pot in front of me with the spoon in the other hand. "Don't you dare touch me, Cindy Nelson, or you'll be sorry, sorry, sorry."

Her eyes blazed with anger but I could tell she was afraid of me. It was a great feeling. I guess it went to my head.

"Wait'll I tell your mother," she screamed. "You'll get it. You wait and see."

"You just bet I'll wait," I told her. "But for now you just get out of our house. You're fired."

She had collected her things and a little dignity. "You can't fire me," she said with her mouth all pulled out of shape. "And you're going to be sorry."

"You're the one who's going to be sorry. This is James's house, not yours. He has a perfect right to use that phone any time he wants to." It wasn't that I meant to steal Bugs's words, but they were right there in my mind because they'd never left since he first said them. "You're mean, that's what you are. How do you think it feels to my little brother to be treated like dirt? You won't even say his name. You don't care what happens to him. You don't even half watch him. You're mean and heartless and lazy and I hate you." Suddenly I ran out of words, or almost did. I glared at her. "Besides, your hair looks like a witch wig."

She stared at me, made some moist, helpless noises with her mouth, and spun toward the door.

I reached it first. It was funny to see her squeeze back as if she thought I would hit her. I had forgotten I was still holding the spoon.

"Be my guest," I said, swinging the door wide. "And don't bother ever coming back."

I closed the door after her and turned around. James was gone. Who in the world had he needed to call that badly? I knew he had gone off to use another phone. That was all right. This was his house. He sure had more right to use the phone here than that Cindy Nelson did.

Suddenly, I was exhausted all over, as tired as if I had played a tennis tournament clear to seven-all and a sudden death. I dragged myself back to the sink and started to set the pot on the counter.

I stared at it in horror. Maybe I had played my own sudden death without even knowing it. The shining red surface of Mom's favorite cooking pot was scarred all over with deep dents. The silvery-colored lining under the finish was shining through. I moaned out loud to myself and stumbled back to slump onto a stool.

This was not my day. It hadn't been my week. I wasn't even sure it was my life. I did know for sure that I couldn't deal with Mom seeing that pot all banged up in the middle of everything else that was going on. I pulled a lot of stuff out of the bottom of the pantry and hid the pot down under the box of freezer containers and the stack of grocery bags we save for trash.

I didn't hear James come back in. He just spoke quietly behind me.

"Thanks anyway, Kate," he said.

"Anyway?" I asked, turning to him. "What's the matter? Didn't you make your phone call?"

When he nodded, the tears began again. "It was too late. I got something called an answer ling surface."

I stared at him. This was the kid who could repeat anything he heard once. Answer ling surface — that could only be an answering service! I slid off the stool. This kid was suddenly beyond me. Who in the world could he be calling?

"Is there anything I can do to help?" I asked.

He shook his head. "It was too late."

He looked awfully little and skinny as he turned and went upstairs. He trailed his hand along the banister and sniffed twice before he even got to the landing.

I followed him upstairs for one more good try. His door was half open. He was under his covers holding that miserable frog up against his cheek and staring toward the window. But at least he had quit crying.

Somehow this all had to make sense. And it had all started with the upside-down boat and that big black Newfoundland fighting for his life. If James *had* seen a man get away, that man had to be someone with a hearing defect because of the orange leash. Nobody had ever said anything about

Andy's hearing but Mom and Dad had mentioned health problems. Andy had gone off to some special school far away when we have both public and private schools right in the area.

But if Andy Wallace had gotten out of that boat and was up there at his house, living with his dog, and having visits with James, why didn't he let anybody know?

The phone call was the scary part. It had been too important to James that he had failed to get through. There had to be some way I could help. Anybody who had an answering service had a home number, too. I looked at the clock. Mom and Dad couldn't possibly get home in less than twenty minutes. All I had to do was get to Andy Wallace. I was almost sure now he was at the Roberts' house.

I put my wraps on and called up the stairs to James. I told him that I'd be back right away and started off for the Roberts' estate.

11. FoJo

The sun eased down behind the ridge just as I let myself out. So maybe I only had eighteen minutes instead of twenty before my folks got home. I started down Ridge Road at a jog to save time. As I passed the Lathrop house the house cleaner's blue van turned out of the Roberts' drive and started toward me. Remembering the morning the driver had almost hit me, I got off the road and cut across the lawn. I needn't have worried. The van slowed down and crept slowly toward the road that led down from the ridge.

Once inside the Roberts' gates, darkness seemed to settle in. I ran up the drive and went straight to the front door. I pulled on the door pull. A hollow, muffled bell sounded inside. Then I remembered about Andy Wallace maybe having trouble hearing. I pulled the gong hard, a whole lot of times in a row. When there still wasn't any answer, I went over and tried to look into the living room window. It was too dark inside the house for me to see anything but vague shapes.

That was when the first doubt hit me. How could anyone, even Andy Wallace, who had known this house since he was a child, manage to live in there without lights? But if there was a light on anywhere in the massive house, it was hidden behind drapes.

I could feel my eighteen minutes ticking away in my head. If Andy had the dog, maybe he kept him out back. Maybe he was out there with the dog right at that moment.

I circled the house, looking for a sign of light in one of the upper windows. When I saw none, I started out back. I had just pushed open the door to the carriage house when I saw dim car lights creeping up the drive. The headlights weren't all the way on but instead were partly lit, as if for parking. They still blinded me enough that it took me a minute to realize it was the blue van.

For no reason at all, I was completely terrified. My heart banged hard against my ribs, and I shivered all over. By the time the van got near the carriage house, I was frozen there just inside the door.

The man at the wheel called out to me. "Hey, kid," he said. "What are you doing up here?"

It had already passed through my mind that the cleaning people knew that Andy Wallace was there. The anger in the man's voice scared me enough that I didn't say who I had come to see.

"Speak up, kid," he said. "You know you're trespassing. You looking for something?"

I jumped on it. "My dog," I stammered. "My dog ran away. I thought he might be up here."

He didn't say anything for a minute but opened the van door and got out. I wanted him to get back in. He was an older man, heavily built, with gray hair cut too close to his head right above his ears. His eyes were small and very intent on mine, and he didn't look as if he even knew how to smile. "Is he a big dog?" he asked. "Black?"

"That's the one," I said, hoping he wouldn't hear my teeth chattering. The way he kept looking at me made me wish I was standing out in the open instead of there with my back to the carriage house door. Then he glanced around, back toward the house, and seemed to relax. "One like that was hanging around this afternoon," he said. "Haven't seen him for hours."

He waited and I did, too.

"Okay, kid," he said. "I'm not leaving here until you scat off this property. Come on, now, get going."

"But, sir," I began.

"Don't give me that," he said. "Get going right now. I want to see you off this property."

I hated his voice as much as I did his face. Sometimes I see an ad for a movie on TV and even though I know I wouldn't watch that movie for anything, the pictures from it stick in my mind when I want to go to sleep. His was that kind of face, one you would try to forget but not be able to. "I'm waiting," he said, his tone threatening. "You want me to call the cops?"

That was all I needed. "No thanks," I said for no good reason except that Mom is really into pushing manners. It was awful to walk down that drive and know he was standing there beside that blue van, watching me. When I got to the road, I started running. Dad's car was just turning into the drive when I reached home.

Mom went on in but Dad waited for me. "Hi, Kate," he called. "Where's James?"

"Inside," I told him. "I just went out for a minute."

"You want to tell him to bring his bike in?" Dad asked.

I hadn't even noticed that James's bike was still lying in the snowbank out in front where he had thrown it. "I'll bring it in," I said, picking my way over to it.

"That's nice of you, Kate," he said. He probably didn't realize how surprised he sounded.

"I can be pretty nice when I think I might get a hug for it," I told him as I lifted James's bike onto its rack.

He laughed and caught me by the shoulders. "You could have had *this* hug for free," he said.

I clung to him, needing his warm strength around me after being yelled at up on the hill. But I knew the evening could still turn dangerous. Spaghetti wasn't the only thing Mom cooked in that red pot.

The phone rang before Mom even got her coat hung up. She answered it, then turned to me with a strange look. "It's for James," she said. "Would you call him to the phone?" Then she added, almost to herself, "Who in the world would be calling James?"

James was still lying on his bed with the frog. He turned over, stared at me, then ran for the phone in Mom and Dad's bedroom. I couldn't help listening to his half of the conversation because I was right there in the hall. Eavesdropping didn't do me very much good. He said "Hello" so softly it's a wonder the caller heard it. Then he nodded and said, "Yes, sir. That's right, sir." Then he smiled from ear to ear and told the caller "goodbye."

When he passed me in the hall going back into his room for his frog, he smiled again — this time at me. He looked better than he had for days, happier somehow. "What's for dinner?" he asked.

I shrugged. "Let's go down and see. I brought in your bike," I told him as we walked downstairs. His glance was apprehensive.

"No problem," I told him. He skipped the rest of the way down the stairs two at a time.

One of Dad's specialties is broiled chicken with sauce from a bottle poured over it right at the last. It's really good with a baked potato and sour cream. I volunteered to do dishes. I was going to need a lot of points marked up in my favor if Mom found her pot before I told her about it.

Bugs called just as I was finishing up. He was too excited to remember that he didn't like me anymore.

"Guess what, Kate," he said. "James *did* see a man down at Smuggler's Spit. I got a picture of him through the cornstalks when I was taking shots of the geese. I couldn't believe it when I picked up my pictures."

"Is it somebody you've seen before?" I said, not wanting to say Andy Wallace's name out loud.

"I'm not sure," he said, hesitating. "He's all bent over as if he were hiding from something. I'll bring it by in the morning."

I don't think anyone knows for sure when the fire started. James tugged me awake. "Please," he begged, his hands hot and sticky on my bare arms. "Wake up, Sissy. Do something."

I snapped at him, more out of habit than anything else. "Kate," I corrected him. "Go back to bed."

His voice was a wail of anguish. "But look, Sissy. Look."

I shoved him away and had started to turn my back on him. Then I saw the fluttering paleness beyond my window. The night sky boiling with raising smoke. I've never waked up that fast in my whole life. I don't remember hitting the floor on the way to the window. I was just there, pressing my forehead against the cold glass, staring in disbelief. The first scarlet tongues of flame licked up, making silhouettes of the chimneys of the Roberts' house. That fire, flickering above the tops of the trees, brought something like a sob into my throat.

"Mom!" I cried, pushing James out of my way. "Dad!"

James caught at me the way little kids do, grabbing me just above the knees so that he almost brought me down. His eyes were pouring out tears and he gasped instead of getting words out. He was clearly going to be a lot of help. "Get dressed," I told him. "Put on something warm."

"FoJo!" he wailed. "My friend. We've got to get them out."

"Get dressed," I repeated, slamming out into the hall.

Mom's voice answered groggily to my knock but Dad was at the door in a moment, still groping for the right sleeve of his robe.

"The Roberts' house," I told him. "There's a fire over there."

"Fire!" Mom squeaked from the bed. "Kate, where's James?"

"I told him to get dressed," I told her, starting back to my own room to do the same. I already heard Dad on the bedroom phone calling the fire department. He kept giving the same directions over and over with rising impatience in his voice.

James was gone from my room, and I figured he had minded for once. I pulled on thermal socks and jeans with a sweatshirt and my down jacket. At the last minute I grabbed my angora earmuffs. Dad was sort of dressed when I got downstairs. He had on trousers and a ski sweater but a striped pajama leg peeked out above his boots. He was in the study, cramming papers into briefcases. One big leather case was already filled by the door and he was still going.

When I reached the kitchen, James was on the phone, standing on tiptoe and shouting about the fire. Mom had clattered down the stairs after me, her face all wadded up with concern. She looked at James, puzzled, just as he thrust the receiver at her. "Here," he said. "He wants to talk to you."

She listened in disbelief, then nodded. "Yes, that's right. They've been called."

She put the phone back and stared at me. "That was Jason Hardaway, Mrs. Roberts's lawyer," she said. "I don't have any idea what's going on." She looked around with a sudden air of panic. "Where did James get to?"

"He probably went to get dressed," I said.

"Check on him, will you, Kate? He's such a little guy."

12. Out of the Woods

I ran upstairs, figuring James was getting dressed. I called but he didn't answer. Where to look? I checked his room and the bathroom and my own room. Nothing.

On the way back downstairs I felt a little panicky myself. What had made me think that James would mind for once? But he *couldn't* have gone outside in the cold wearing nothing but his sleepers with feet in them.

He couldn't be in the kitchen or study because Mom and Dad were there. I let myself out on the porch to check the front yard. Already I heard sirens wailing along the river road from Northville. The air was clotted with black shreds spinning like confetti, and the noise was awful — not just one sound but a lot of different ones. The hungry crackling and crunching were the worst. The fire sounded like some ravenous beast gobbling up the world.

As I yelled for James, I knew the clatter and

whine of the fire trucks racing up the hill drowned out my voice.

Dad had backed both cars out and was loading things into the back of the station wagon. Mom flew out the back door and wailed at him just the way James does at me. "How can you do that? How can you worry about *things* when Kate and I can't find James?"

"He's around," Dad called. "I just saw him. We may have to be ready to move out of here in a hurry if need be."

Only then did I realize what he was doing. He was packing the things he couldn't spare. I just stared at him. What did I have that I couldn't spare? A lot of stuff fluttered through my head: clothes, tapes, pictures, my tennis racket, and maybe my pastels.

Dad glanced over at me. "Do your mom a favor, Kate," he said. "Find James."

What had James said up in my room when he woke me up? "FoJo. My friend. We've got to get them out." FoJo didn't make any sense, but the friend could be Andy Wallace. Could that crazy kid be on his way to the Roberts' house in his pajamas?

"I'm going to look down the road," I called to Dad, setting off running.

"Be careful," he called after me. "Don't get too close, and come right back."

Cars were still grinding up the road from town,

police cars with their lights splashing the woods with color, and regular cars, strange cars. I stumbled along the edge of the road, afraid I wouldn't hear a car behind me with all the noise from the fire. The firemen really moved fast. I heard them shouting at each other over the hissing of their hoses and the monstrous sickening crackle of burning wood. A sort of a van with a giant antenna passed me, stopped, and a man leaned out. "Hey, kid," he shouted. "Is it the Roberts' place?"

I nodded and hurried on. He called the name of a local TV station and asked me to come over. I shook my head. "I can't," I told him. "I'm looking for someone."

"In the fire?" he asked, his voice rising as if he enjoyed the idea. "We understood the place was vacant."

"It is," I said, cutting across the Lathrops' yard to get away from him. All the neighbors were up and out, standing in their drives, their faces looking bleached from watching. I wondered if Bugs Moran was out in front of his house down at the end of the ridge.

Like Dad, the Lathrops had loaded their car. They must have gotten tired because they were just standing beside it, staring. "What happened, Kate?" Mrs. Lathrop asked.

I couldn't look at her because I wouldn't have wanted anyone to look at me when I was dressed that way. Something dark and webby-looking covered all her gray hair. It was knotted so tightly over her right ear that it cut a dark line across her forehead just above her eyes. Her face was streaked as if she had been crying and her robe must have belonged to Mr. Lathrop because it was too ugly a gray and too long for a woman.

"I don't know," I said. "We just saw it and Dad called the firehouse."

She glanced toward the billowing flames, covering her mouth with her fingers. Mr. Lathrop touched her arm. "They'll control it, wait and see. Just pray it doesn't take the house."

She whimpered something, but I looked up, startled. Mr. Lathrop was right, the fire *wasn't* in the house. That's why the chimneys had been silhouetted like that. The fire was behind the house, in the stables or maybe the carriage house.

Then I got the bright idea. None of those grown-ups were going to let me in there to look for James. I had to sneak in from the forest preserve side behind the fire. I cut through Mrs. Mclaughlin's backyard and was just starting toward the Roberts' house when I heard Bugs.

"Kate!" he shouted. "Wait up." He was running toward me from the other side of the Roberts' place. I could have grinned. Bugs and I may not have great minds but they sure run on a single track.

He was there in seconds. "You haven't seen James, have you?" I asked. "He's disappeared."

Bugs looked toward the hissing, raging inferno that had been the Roberts' stables and carriage house. His face looked sick in the weird, uneven light of the flames. "He can't be there," he said, shaking his head violently.

"He was looking for someone — or something," I corrected myself. "What could FoJo mean?"

He didn't look at me but kept staring at the fire. His words came in that "walking en-cyclopedia" tone that usually makes me furious. "It's a bay, maybe an island, too. In New Found-land." His eyes widened and he stared at me. "FoJo. Newfoundland. Kate! That dog was a Newfie."

The wind shifted, bringing a blast of hot air our way. I turned my back on the fire and held up my arm to shield my face. The wind must have un-balanced something on the roof of the carriage house. It suddenly collapsed, sending a great plume of light upward and filling the sky with a shower of sparks.

I heard Bugs gasp and felt him grab my arm. He started running into the forest preserve, dragging me along behind him. As I stumbled after him, I looked ahead, and my knees almost gave away. Three figures stood silent and un-moving in the shadow of a grove only a few yards away. The man was tall and bareheaded, and he seemed to be supporting himself by a gnarled stick at his side. Pressed against him was a skinny little figure in light pajamas, and a giant black dog.

"James," I cried, breaking away from Bugs to race toward him. I hadn't cried. In spite of that sob that caught in my throat at the first sign of smoke, I hadn't cried the way Mrs. Lathrop had. At the sight of James, my eyes filled up, and tears spilled all down my face, making it sting in the smoky air.

"James," I cried. "James."

The dog began to bark but the tall man laid his hand on his back and quieted him.

"I found them," James cried, gripping the back of the neck of the animal and looking up at Andy Wallace. "They're both okay. I found them."

Andy Wallace looked different close up. He needed a shave something awful, and his face looked tight, as if he hurt somewhere. "You two must be okay," he said thoughtfully. Then he smiled. "Any friend of this little guy's is my friend, too."

I started to answer but he shook his head. "I'm sorry. I can't even hear thunder until I get some help."

"Mr. Hardaway has had new ears made for Andy," James said. "He's coming right away. I called him."

"How about we go down by the road where Mr. Hardaway can find you?" asked Bugs, always the voice of reason.

James stared at him, then turned and tugged on Andy's arm. The tall man smiled and said, "Got to trust my friend here."

Andy Wallace walked painfully, leaning heavily on his stick. "Some man tried to shoot him in the parking lot," James told us. "He hurt his leg running away."

"But he got to the boat," I said.

James shook his head. "Oh, no, he didn't. He got here through the woods."

"He's right," Bugs said. "This isn't the man whose picture I took down on Smuggler's Spit."

This was all too much for me to grasp at once with the crazy fire noises in the background. "Let's get home," I told James. "Mom's having a conniption. Why did you run off like that?"

"I was afraid Andy wouldn't hear the fire," James said. "It was all right, though. FoJo warned him to get out in time."

"Do you know what's going on?" I asked Bugs.

"Warning their masters of danger is what Hearing Dogs are all about," he said, running ahead to open Mrs. Mclaughlin's gate and hold it for the rest of us.

Dad and Mom were standing with Jason Hardaway in the bushes on the other side of Ridge Road. They saw us the minute we came around Mrs. Mclaughlin's house. Mom began crying helplessly as she ran toward us. "James," Mom cried, hugging him against her. Then she was sort of grabbing at all of us. "Kate, Bugs, Andy."

"And this is FoJo," James said, wriggling loose. "Isn't he beautiful?" He knelt and put both arms around the animal, who thumped his big plume of a tail against my leg. It isn't that I dislike dogs; it's just that they can be so gross. This one was panting. Huge swinging drops of spittle landed on James's pajama top and ran down his arm.

Jason Hardaway talked quietly to Andy Wallace after Andy fitted something into his ears. Andy looked up and smiled. "Hey, fellow," he called to James.

I was so used to correcting Cindy that it popped right out. "His name is James," I told him.

He looked at me as if he were really pleased. "Thanks, I really wondered. Hey, James!"

"Yeah, Andy?" James said, looking up.

"You got the license number on that van absolutely right. The police located it right away." He turned to Mom and Dad. "I can't believe your son's memory."

"But what about the man in it?" James asked. "The one who stole all the art things out of your house?"

"No luck on him yet," Andy said. "But they are still trying."

Mr. Hardaway turned to my folks. "This all must look very strange to you. Andy had an attempt made on his life. He managed to get home but didn't know who he could trust. He had lost his hearing aid and had an injured leg. Even if he had a phone, he would have had trouble using it." He grinned. "James befriended him and became our go-between."

"You talked about art being stolen," Dad said. "Couldn't you have put a police guard up there?"

"It was more important to me to find out who the thief was," Andy told him. "That way we had a fighting chance to recover some of those treasures."

"You've had a rough week, Andy," Mom said. "What a welcome home!"

"It has been," Jason Hardaway agreed. "But thanks to James, he made it through. Now if you would excuse me, I need to check on the progress of that fire. It looks as if they've finally contained it."

"We don't need to stand out here," Mom told him. "We'll be down at the house." She turned to Andy. "You must be starving!"

Andy Wallace smiled just the way his grandmother did. In fact, he looked a lot like her except for the beard. "My friend James took care of me. Heaven knows where he got all those cookies and peanut butter," he paused. "I *could* use a cup of coffee, come to think of it."

While the coffee was brewing, Mom looked down at FoJo, who was creating a small lake of spit on her polished kitchen floor. "What about something for your dainty friend, James?" she asked.

The minute James sneaked that guilty look at me, the truth hit me.

"Should I go bring some kibble from Mrs. Mclaughlin's garage for your friend?" I asked sweetly.

"Andy and I will pay Mrs. Mclaughlin all back," James said quickly, his face turning very pale. "And, Mom, we'll pay you back for the stuff I took from here, too, won't we Andy?"

Mom was too horrified to speak, but Bugs and I both broke up laughing. I could still remember my goose pimples when I stood in that garage *knowing* something was wrong but not able to guess what. James would never know what a chill he had put into me!

We would have explained why it was so funny but right then Jason Hardaway came back to say that, indeed, the fire was "contained, and already the police suspect arson from the peculiar pattern of the development of the fire."

13. Bugs

Dawn was streaking the sky when Captain Logan arrived just minutes after Mr. Hardaway. "Technically we should do this down at the station," he told Dad. "But to be honest, that place still stinks from the flood. We got about two feet of Wolf River when that levee broke."

"After what Andy's been through, this is better," Mom said, setting a fresh pot of coffee on the low table in the family room.

"And I want to hear what really happened," Dad said.

"*I* know," James piped up.

Andy laughed and nudged him with his foot. "This James is my little lifesaver right here. And is it great to have it all over with!"

"It's not over until we get the guy who tried to shoot you," Captain Logan reminded him.

"You must have a suspect!" Dad said.

"I do, but suspicion isn't enough," Mr. Hardaway said unhappily. "Right after Andy's grandmother died, his Uncle Clovis Roberts's business associates started coming to me asking about her will. They weren't what you'd call savory types, and it was plain that Clovis had borrowed heavily against this inheritance. The truth was that the only way Clovis could touch that money was if Andy were dead. You can see why I got worried about Andy's safety."

"That's when Jason cabled me," Andy said. "He didn't mention any danger. He just said he had made me a reservation at the inn, and I was to stay there until he reached me. He said he'd have Frimmle clean the yard, and have the house readied. I just thought he was really going overboard being kind."

"I wasn't careful enough," Hardaway admitted. "I shouldn't have let anyone know that Andy was coming. I should have registered him at the inn under a false name."

"We don't know when the assailant started watching that parking lot," Captain Logan said. "But the blue van was reported late Saturday and all day Sunday, when Andy was expected. Nobody realized anyone was in the van with those darkened windows. Now we realize that the van was only rented because we located it after it was returned."

"I might have gotten to the inn as early as Saturday if I hadn't stopped in Denver to pick up

FoJo. He is my last gift from Granny. She had him trained and waiting for my return."

"Tell us what happened from the time you reached the inn," Captain Logan said, his notebook on his knee.

"To be honest, I never knew what hit me. I parked the car and got out. I stretched, then let FoJo out and hooked his lead over the door handle to keep him from wandering away. Then I went around to get my bags out of the car trunk.

"Suddenly the town went crazy. Sirens screamed, people shouted, and FoJo lunged toward me, barking wildly. I thought the noise scared him and tried to hurry back to him. Instead, he was trying to warn me that someone was behind me. I felt a stunning, swift blow to my head. It pitched me forward into the trunk of the car." Andy grinned at Bugs and me.

"I've been in some strange situations in my work. You develop quick reactions. I grabbed my suitcase and swung it around, hitting the man hard in the midriff. When he went down with his gun still trained on me, I panicked."

"Did you recognize him?" Bugs asked.

Andy shook his head. "I know I've never seen that man before in my life. I took off running, dodging off between cars, figuring I could get help." He shook his head. "The levee had broken. Water coursed through the lot, which was suddenly full of people trying to get their cars moved. I didn't see the concrete block under the swirling water. I ran right into it and went down hard. I thought I'd broken my leg as well as splitting my head open and losing my glasses that have my hearing aids in them. I know now it was only a bad sprain, but there was no question of running. By the time I got to my feet, I had lost sight of the man with the gun."

"Your assailant grabbed your luggage and set it inside the door of the Inn," Captain Logan said. "When you got back on your feet and looked around, was your rented car still there?"

Andy shook his head. "Not where it had been. When I did finally see it, the man with the gun was in it at the edge of the lot by the river and FoJo was gone. I couldn't hear a thing after that fall. My forehead was bleeding, and I was plastered with mud. The water was rising steadily. It was halfway to my knees. I saw people shouting, and knew the place was a madhouse, but I heard nothing. I grabbed a guy, trying to tell him about the car, but he shook me off, shouting something."

I glanced over at Bugs, knowing he was thinking what I was. The thought of *knowing* there was sound going on all around you and hearing nothing made me shiver.

"I saw the river swirl over the top of the car but could do nothing. The water in the lot was deep enough to pull at my injured leg, almost dragging me down. As I turned away I saw the rowboat swing out into the current. The man was in it with FoJo lying in the bottom of the boat as if he were dead. The flood in the lot was getting worse by the minute. I limped up the street to the first public phone I could find. I called the police and reported what had happened." Andy glanced at Captain Logan.

"So *you* were the anonymous caller," the policeman said. "But you just repeated you'd seen a man in a boat over and over and then hung up. You didn't answer our questions or tell us where you sighted this boat."

"I couldn't *hear* you," Andy reminded him. "I wasn't even sure I'd reached anyone." He grinned. "And I was afraid. I didn't know who this man was or why he was after me."

"Couldn't you just catch a policeman and ask him to help?" I asked.

Andy grinned at me. "Kate, you can't imagine what a nightmare that place was. The lower part of town was being evacuated. There were rowboats in the street and an air of crisis all around my silence. I couldn't hear or even prove who I was. My wallet with all my identification was at the bottom of the river in that car. I didn't know who could be trusted. Of course, Jason knew where I was, and Frimmle did. I had agreed to meet a man from Ponti Builders so he knew I was

111

there. I've never felt so helpless in my entire life. I was cold, my leg and my head both hurt. I simply cut west toward high ground, thinking that if I could get home to the ridge, I could figure out something."

"But how could you walk on that sprain?" Mom asked.

"Like a hermit in a book," Andy said. "With a tree limb as a cane and stopping every few minutes to feel sorry for myself."

James broke in. "Andy walked all night in the woods and slept in the stable. He sneaked into the house when Mr. Frimmle unlocked it to get out the tools."

Andy nodded. "Then came the second shock. As I went through the house, newly cleaned for my arrival, I saw that the most valuable pieces in my collection were missing. I knew that Granny would never have parted with them. Hundreds of thousands of dollars worth of art had simply disappeared. I realized that whoever had raided the house had probably attacked me, too."

"I hadn't remembered to hook up the telephone," Jason Hardaway said. "Andy was trapped there, unable to get help." Then he smiled at James. "Until he found his friend James, who could bring him food, call me for help, and report the license number on that van."

Bugs had sat silent for a long time. He stood up, fished something out of his back pocket, and handed it to Andy Wallace. "Was this the man who tried to shoot you?" he asked.

Andy Wallace stared at the picture and then at Bugs. "It's him," he cried. "That's the man. Where did you get this?"

"I took it the afternoon we rescued the dog. I was concentrating so hard on that big goose that I didn't even notice the background. Then the pictures came back and there he was."

Everyone crowded around Andy. "That's the man who was driving the blue van last night," I said. "The one who chased me away from the carriage house."

"That is Clovis Roberts," Mr. Hardaway said, his voice suddenly weak and strange.

"All right," Captain Logan leaped to his feet. "Now we're in business. We impounded the van from the rental agency he leased it from. We can check it for fingerprints and any other physical evidence. May I use the phone in your kitchen?"

At the doorway he turned. "I don't understand why you didn't recognize him if he's your own father's brother."

Andy shook his head. "There was no love lost between my father and Uncle Clovis. I never saw him all the years I was growing up."

Mom invited everyone to stay and have breakfast with us, but nobody took her up on it. Mr. Hardaway insisted that Andy and FoJo come home with him for some decent sleep. Captain Logan was halfway to his cruiser before he could finish saying, "No, thanks."

Bugs's mother called up angry for the first time since we've been friends. "She can live with me coming home late," Bugs explained. "Staying out all night she's not ready for."

Mom made us pancakes out of a box. When James went to sleep with his face in his plate, she called in to have both of us excused from school.

14. The Final Question

As I said, the only mystery in the beginning was how I could have been so totally stupid as to take James down by Wolf River that March Monday.

All the other mysteries that surfaced were finally explained. When James went looking for FoJo that first night, he had found both the dog and Andy in the stable. The very next day the little kid started raiding our house and Mrs. Mclaughlin's to feed Andy and FoJo. Thanks to Bugs's picture, Clovis Roberts was apprehended (I love that word and must remember to use it when I am a mystery writer). The rented blue van had Clovis Roberts's fingerprints all over it. He was stopped leaving the Chicago area in a rented car with Andy's priceless Chinese camels wrapped up in the trunk.

I guess nobody will ever know the answer to the last remaining question. If Bugs and James and I had not been down on Smuggler's Spit to see FoJo drowning, would Clovis Roberts have done away with Andy Wallace with no one ever finding out? We knew by Bugs's picture that Clovis had crawled to shore before we hauled the dog in. He still had that rented blue van parked somewhere, and Andy was helpless up there with no hearing aid or phone.

It's better this way, even after all the scary stuff. I would never have taken enough of a look at James to see what he was really like. He really won't be all that bad if he ever sprouts teeth. And he's not boring!

And certainly we would not have all been invited to the Roberts' house that Saturday night to see Andy's big stone parlor fireplace filled with crackling logs. It looked like a Christmas card except there weren't any stockings hanging up. The rug in front of the fire looked like a Christmas card, too, with FoJo stretched out beside James. Both the boy and the dog *looked* sound asleep, but I knew better about James anyway.

Captain Logan glowed with success and loved answering the questions Bugs and I couldn't answer for ourselves. "Dumping the car was an easy enough trick for Clovis Roberts to pull. He probably jumped out just as the car slid down that muddy embankment."

"But the boat?" Andy asked. "Where did he get the boat?"

"Again, no problem. A half dozen old rowboats are always tied down by that ramp. What Clovis didn't realize was that the owners take their oars home to discourage thieves."

"That Clovis Roberts is *really* a mean man," James put in. "He didn't have to give FoJo that lump on the head and put him in the boat."

"Roberts probably thought he did. Andy had to appear to have died in the flood. That's why Clovis set Andy's bag inside the Inn. He meant to finish Andy off one way or another. He depended on the river either to drown the dog or carry him too far downstream to be associated with himself or Andy Wallace."

"Then you figure Clovis was aiming for Smuggler's Spit all the time?" Dad asked.

Captain Logan nodded. "Very probably. Where else would Andy be likely to go? And don't forget, Clovis grew up on this ridge. He knows that river as well as your kids do."

I felt Mom glance at me but I didn't look up. But I was still glad she heard it. I may be disobedient, but I'm not strange.

Andy leaned to stroke FoJo's head, his hand lingering on the goose egg on the dog's forehead. FoJo whimpered softly and pulled away. Andy Wallace looked over at me and grinned. "Do you think James will ever grow up to that dog?"

"Big isn't everything," Bugs said without opening his eyes. He was sitting on the floor, too, leaning back against the divan. With his glasses off, he looked really young and sort of unfinished.

"It sure isn't," Andy said, leaning over to shove Bugs's billed cap down over his eyes. "Jason and I might have lost this gamble if it hadn't been for you kids. I'd have lost FoJo anyway."

The dog must have been only half asleep, too, because his tail thumped a couple of times at the sound of his name. But like Bugs, he didn't bother opening his eyes.

"James was the hero," Bugs protested.

"But it wouldn't have worked without the picture you took," I reminded him.

Mom and Dad had been awfully quiet. "Now what, Andy?" Dad asked. "Will you rebuild the carriage house and stables?"

Andy was so slow to answer that I wasn't sure he had heard Dad. But he had. "I have to give you a yes and no on that," he said finally. "Obviously this place is too big for me to use as a home for myself. Still, I have to stay somewhere until I'm really back on my feet again."

"We'll take care of you here," James said sleepily.

"I know you would, James. And I'm not half tired of cookies and peanut butter. Ponti Builders have made a very handsome offer for this place. To be honest, I was really considering it until I was forced to hide out here. This house had gotten to me. It's full of memories of my grandparents, even of my mother growing up here. I'd hate to see it fall to a wrecker's ball or be hemmed in with other houses."

Jason Hardaway crossed his legs and sighed. "Andrew has a crazy idea that might not fly. If it does, the property will stay the way it is. If it doesn't . . ." His voice trailed off.

"Hey, you two," Dad said. "Haven't we had more than enough mysteries on this hill in the last week? What's the idea?"

"Dogs," Andrew Wallace said bluntly. "There's plenty of space for a training facility here for dogs like FoJo. According to Hardaway, I can afford the luxury of a hobby that will do some good."

"Why wouldn't it fly?" I asked.

Mr. Wallace laughed. "This area is zoned for residential use only. Getting a permit to build dog runs and training facilities out there where the stables were might be a problem."

"Who could object?" I asked.

"Anyone who lives up here on the ridge," Mr. Hardaway replied. "I've seen whole neighborhoods blown apart over zoning exceptions like this one would be."

Bugs was suddenly wide awake with his glasses perched on his nose. "Kate and I will take care of that."

I stared at him.

"Come on," he said. "There's only the Lathrops, Mrs. Mclaughlin, and the Nelsons to convince."

"You take the Nelsons," I said quickly. The other two would be easy. As scared of everything as the Lathrops are, they would jump at the chance to have a lot of good dogs on the hill. Mrs. Mclaughlin is like Bugs; she likes any creature that flies or creeps or crawls.

Mom frowned, looking confused. "The Nelsons," Mom said suddenly. "That reminds me. Hasn't Cindy been leaving bills for me? Or are there this many swim meets?"

"Kate fired her," James said in a tone of vast satisfaction.

I felt my face flush scarlet as everyone in that whole room turned to stare at me. Bugs was maybe the worst. His mouth hung open in complete astonishment. "She *what?*" Dad asked James with disbelief.

"Cindy wouldn't let me use the phone to call Mr. Hardaway and give him the license number of the blue van," James said. "Kate banged on Mom's red pot until Cindy gave up. Then Kate told Cindy not to come back unless she could treat me like I was human and watch me better."

Mom's tone was scary. "You said that, Kate?"

I figured that if I was going to get in trouble, I might as well get in good and deep. "James can't help it if he's still learning to be a person. And that doesn't give her the license to treat him like dirt. But don't worry. I'm going to take care of him. I don't mind having him tag around after me." Then I grinned. "In fact, I'd rather have him tag around after me than try to figure where he's off to on his own."

"I'm around, too," Bugs put in quickly, still with his eyes shut. "I can help."

"With any luck at all, I'll be here to back the kids up," Andrew Wallace said. "FoJo and I both."

"There are rules," Mom said sternly, looking around at all of us.

James rolled over on his stomach and looked right at Mom. "We *only* went down to the cornfield, not the river," he told her patiently.

I know I shouldn't have laughed but it slipped out. Then everyone was chuckling, even Mom.

Andy Wallace looked around the room. "Isn't anybody hungry but me? Now that we finally have a phone, I think we need to break in the pizza delivery people as to where this place is."

Jason Hardaway rose and pulled a pad off the desk. "Orders?" he asked.

"Do they make a peanut butter pizza?" James asked wistfully.

I glanced at Bugs. He was grinning at me with his nose squinched up in wonderful, hideous revulsion.

This from a guy who plays with spiders?

About the Author

MARY FRANCIS SHURA has written over twenty books for young readers, including the prize-winning *The Josie Gambit* (an ALA Notable Book for 1986); *The Sunday Doll* (a Junior Literary Guild Selection); *The Search for Grissi*, which received the 1985 Carl Sandburg Literary Arts Award for Children's Literature; and the three companion books *Chester*, *Eleanor*, and *Jefferson*, the first two of which were selected for Children's Choices by the International Reading Association/Children's Book Council Joint Committee. Ms. Shura is also the author of five historical novels in Scholastic's *Sunfire* series, most recently finishing *Darcy* about a girl caught in the Galveston Hurricane of 1900.

Ms. Shura has four grown children, and now makes her home near Chicago, where she enjoys tennis, chess, reading, and cooking when she is not writing. She is currently working on a series for younger readers for Scholastic.

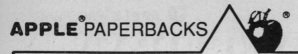

APPLE® PAPERBACKS

Pick an Apple and Polish Off Some Great Reading!

BEST-SELLING APPLE TITLES

❏ MT43944-8 **Afternoon of the Elves** Janet Taylor Lisle		$2.75
❏ MT43109-9 **Boys Are Yucko** Anna Grossnickle Hines		$2.95
❏ MT43473-X **The Broccoli Tapes** Jan Slepian		$2.95
❏ MT40961-1 **Chocolate Covered Ants** Stephen Manes		$2.95
❏ MT45436-6 **Cousins** Virginia Hamilton		$2.95
❏ MT44036-5 **George Washington's Socks** Elvira Woodruff		$2.95
❏ MT45244-4 **Ghost Cadet** Elaine Marie Alphin		$2.95
❏ MT44351-8 **Help! I'm a Prisoner in the Library** Eth Clifford		$2.95
❏ MT43618-X **Me and Katie (The Pest)** Ann M. Martin		$2.95
❏ MT43030-0 **Shoebag** Mary James		$2.95
❏ MT46075-7 **Sixth Grade Secrets** Louis Sachar		$2.95
❏ MT42882-9 **Sixth Grade Sleepover** Eve Bunting		$2.95
❏ MT41732-0 **Too Many Murphys** Colleen O'Shaughnessy McKenna		$2.95

Available wherever you buy books, or use this order form.

- -

Scholastic Inc., P.O. Box 7502, 2931 East McCarty Street, Jefferson City, MO 65102

Please send me the books I have checked above. I am enclosing $_____ (please add $2.00 to cover shipping and handling). Send check or money order — no cash or C.O.D.s please.

Name_____ **Birthdate**_____

Address _____

City_____ **State/Zip** _____

Please allow four to six weeks for delivery. Offer good in the U.S.A. only. Sorry, mail orders are not available to residents of Canada. Prices subject to change.

APP693

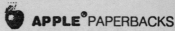
APPLE®PAPERBACKS

ADVENTURE! MYSTERY! ACTION!

Exciting stories for you!

❏ MN42417-3	**The Adventures of the Red Tape Gang**	Joan Lowery Nixon	$2.75
❏ MN41836-X	**Custer and Crazy Horse: A Story of Two Warriors**	Jim Razzi	$2.75
❏ MN44576-6	**Encyclopedia Brown Takes the Cake!** Donald J. Sobol and Glenn Andrews		$2.95
❏ MN42513-7	**Fast-Talking Dolphin**	Carson Davidson	$2.75
❏ MN42463-7	**Follow My Leader**	James B. Garfield	$2.75
❏ MN43534-5	**I Hate Your Guts, Ben Brooster**	Eth Clifford	$2.75
❏ MN44113-2	**Kavik, the Wolf Dog**	Walt Morey	$2.95
❏ MN32197-8	**The Lemonade Trick**	Scott Corbett	$2.95
❏ MN44352-6	**The Loner**	Ester Weir	$2.75
❏ MN41001-6	**Oh, Brother**	Johnniece Marshall Wilson	$2.95
❏ MN43755-0	**Our Man Weston**	Gordon Korman	$2.95
❏ MN41809-2	**Robin on His Own**	Johnniece Marshall Wilson	$2.95
❏ MN40567-5	**Spies on the Devil's Belt**	Betsy Haynes	$2.75
❏ MN43303-2	**T.J. and the Pirate Who Wouldn't Go Home**	Carol Gorman	$2.75
❏ MN42378-9	**Thank You, Jackie Robinson**	Barbara Cohen	$2.95
❏ MN44206-6	**The War with Mr. Wizzle**	Gordon Korman	$2.75
❏ MN44174-4	**The Zucchini Warriors**	Gordon Korman	$2.95

Available wherever you buy books, or use this order form.

Scholastic Inc., P.O. Box 7502, 2931 East McCarty Street, Jefferson City, MO 65102

Please send me the books I have checked above. I am enclosing $_____ (please add $2.00 to cover shipping and handling). Send check or money order — no cash or C.O.D.s please.

Name _____

Address_____

City _____ State/Zip _____

Please allow four to six weeks for delivery. Offer good in the U.S. only. Sorry, mail orders are not available to residents of Canada. Prices subject to change.

AB991